Murder
at the
Margin

Murder
at the
Margin

MARSHALL JEVONS

A Henry Spearman Mystery

PRINCETON UNIVERSITY PRESS
PRINCETON, NEW JERSEY

PUBLISHED BY PRINCETON UNIVERSITY PRESS, 41 WILLIAM STREET
PRINCETON, NEW JERSEY 08540
IN THE UNITED KINGDOM: PRINCETON UNIVERSITY PRESS,
CHICHESTER, WEST SUSSEX

LIBRARY OF CONGRESS CATALOGING-IN-PUBLICATION DATA

JEVONS, MARSHALL.
MURDER AT THE MARGIN: A HENRY SPEARMAN MYSTERY /
MARSHALL JEVONS
P. CM.
ISBN 0-691-03391-9—ISBN 0-691-00098-0 (PBK.)
1. ECONOMISTS—UNITED STATES—FICTION. I. TITLE.
PS3560.E88M87 1993 813'.—DC20 93-19771

FIRST PRINCETON PAPERBACK PRINTING, 1993

PRINCETON UNIVERSITY PRESS BOOKS ARE PRINTED ON
ACID-FREE PAPER AND MEET THE GUIDELINES FOR PERMANENCE AND
DURABILITY OF THE COMMITTEE ON PRODUCTION GUIDELINES FOR BOOK
LONGEVITY OF THE COUNCIL ON LIBRARY RESOURCES

5   7   9   10   8   6

PRINTED IN THE UNITED STATES OF AMERICA

I learn a good deal by merely observing you,
And letting you talk as long as you please,
And taking note of what you do not say.

T. S. Eliot
The Cocktail Party

1/4/2001

Murder at the Margin

EVERY GREAT DETECTIVE has his or her milieu. For Sherlock Holmes it is the dingy streets and stately mansions of Edwardian England. For Miss Marple it is a British country village. For Inspector Maigret it is the boulevards of Paris. Such detectives know not only the geography of these places, they know the institutions and the people as well. They understand how things work in their milieu and how people behave there.

Henry Spearman, the detective-hero of *Murder at the Margin*, has a different kind of milieu, one not confined to any particular time or space. His milieu is inside the head of the rational man or woman, the person who, if given a choice between two ways of achieving a given objective, always chooses the way that costs less. By understanding how such a person would behave, and on the assumption that all the persons involved are rational in that sense, Spearman solves the mystery.

Our detective is an economist. He is a student of rational, goal-maximizing behavior. He also thinks, talks, and acts like a person for whom rationality is constantly foremost in his mind. Moreover, the author, Marshall Jevons, is also an economist. When Henry Spearman neglects to explain adequately the economic analysis that underlies his thinking, the author does it for him.

Spearman, and the author, bring to bear in the course

of solving their mystery a number of economic concepts that are variations on the theme of rationality. There are discussions of the way a rational person thinks about the choice between income-earning work and leisure, about how to set the optimum price for selling a book, about why some people have the relationships to others that they do, about how quantities of products supplied and sold are kept equal, about the impossibility of comparing the utilities of different individuals, and so on.

But this is all incidental to the fact that there have been murders and we don't know who done it. Spearman discovers who done it by rigorous application of a very simple economic proposition, coupled with acute observation. The essence of the plot is that there is a mystery—someone is behaving in a way that is not transparent, but we do not know who it is. When Spearman sees someone behaving in a way that *seems* to be irrational, not the apparent least-cost way of achieving his apparent objective, he knows that there is a mystery about that person. That person has some objective or some costs that are not apparent. And if Spearman has sufficient observations of apparently irrational behavior he can deduce what the person is up to.

Without giving away the denouement of *Murder at the Margin* I can provide a simple, if absurd, illustration that is not in the book. Suppose you see that in your hotel dining room at breakfast a person has a choice between two apparently identical doughnuts, one for fifty cents and one for a dollar. He chooses the one for a dollar. You then deduce that the two doughnuts are not identical to him. But suppose you observe that he had also bought up all the copies of the morning newspaper in the hotel where you both are staying, although a rational person would have been satisfied with one, and you know that the paper had a front-page story about the disappearance of a ruby from the forehead of an Indian idol. You might then deduce that the dollar doughnut contained the Indian ruby.

Murder at the Margin has been used as supplementary reading in many introductory courses in economics. It serves to get the beginning student curious about economic concepts and provides a hook upon which an instructor can hang a more formal lecture. Professional economists will get pleasure from seeing familiar principles used in unfamiliar circumstances. People who know little about economics will learn something of what economics and economists are like.

But *Murder at the Margin* is not an economics textbook and one would no more read it to learn economics than one would read Conan Doyle to learn the chemistry of cigar ashes or Agatha Christie to learn toxicology. The economics is the shtick and not the shtory.

The story is a good classical detective story with all the necessary ingredients well developed. There are murder victims to whom we have no particular attachment. Our interest in the puzzle of who killed them is not alloyed by any sadness at their passing. There are a number of plausible suspects. There are the necessary clues for the solution, hidden in a haystack of circumstance and incident. A sufficiently assiduous, attentive, logical reader might discover the solution before it is revealed, but such a reader would be exceedingly rare. When the highly observant, analytical, and courageous detective reveals the culprit, the reader acknowledges that he has been fairly treated and admires the author's skill. One doesn't have to be an economist to enjoy all that.

There are several mysteries about *Murder at the Margin* in addition to the mystery of who killed whom. The author warns us at the outset that *"Murder at the Margin* is fiction, and all the characters and adventures are imaginary. Any resemblance to actual persons, living or dead, is purely coincidental." Now, such a notice is needed only when a book is so close to the truth that a reader might take it for the truth unless he were warned. So one has to ask what it is about this book that is so much like the truth that the reader might not realize it is fiction.

The first mystery is about the identity of the author, Marshall Jevons, from internal evidence an economist. But there is no economist named "Marshall Jevons." Alfred Marshall was a great economist and so was William Jevons, but one died in 1924 and the other in 1882 so we can safely conclude that this book, first published in 1978, was not the result of a collaboration between them.

That mystery has now been solved. There are two authors, William Breit and Kenneth Elzinga. Elzinga is a professor of economics at the University of Virginia and Breit, formerly at Virginia, is now a professor of economics at Trinity University in San Antonio. Both are excellent economists with outstanding economic writing and teaching experience to their credit. Obviously, both are among the more imaginative and creative members of the profession.

Breit and Elzinga say that they wrote a detective story "for fun." That is a concept that creates difficulty for economists. If one asks why of all the economists who have ever lived only these two wrote a detective story, all economics can tell us is that they were the only two who got more utility out of writing a detective story than out of any other possible use of their time. But this is only a fancy way of stating the obvious.

A deeper mystery is who Henry Spearman is. Many readers have jumped to the conclusion that he is Milton Friedman. They think that because Spearman is a good economist, short, and "balding," one of the authors' favorite words. But Spearman in many important respects is unlike Friedman. Spearman teaches at Harvard, he has a wife who is not an economist and her name, improbably, is "Pidge." Out of the twenty thousand or so economists in the country there must be more than one who is a good economist and also short and "balding." So if there is a real model for Spearman, his identity remains a mystery, at least to me.

Finally, there is a question of how much is real and how much is fiction in the world and persona of Henry Spearman, and what the authors intend for us to think about that. I don't suppose that Conan Doyle and Agatha Christie would have insisted that the worlds of their detectives were totally real worlds. But to what degree the world of total economic rationality described by Spearman and the authors is the real world is still an open question for economists.

At one point in the book there is some talk about why a man who is known to dislike dancing dances with his wife, who is known to like dancing. Someone suggests that the man is in love with his wife. Spearman offers a more "rational economic" explanation, which is that the two have interdependent utility functions, so that the man gets pleasure out of her pleasure. One has to wonder whether anyone talks like that and whether he is adding anything to the explanation beyond the statement that the man is in love with his wife. Are the authors, who wrote the book for fun, having a little fun at the expense of the pretensions of economics?

An economist, it may have been J. M. Clark, once referred scornfully to what he called "the irrational passion for dispassionate rationality." Rationality beyond some point may be not worth the trouble and even counterproductive, taking the "fun" out of life, to return to that word. That there is irrationality in the real world creates a problem for Spearman. He solves the mystery by believing that if someone does something that is apparently irrational there must be a hidden rationality behind it, and he seeks to discover what it is. If the irrationality is truly irrational—if, despite Freud, a cigar may after all be nothing but a cigar—Spearman's methods of detection will not work.

So there are two puzzles in *Murder at the Margin*. One is who killed A and B. The other is how much resemblance the world of rational economics in which the story takes place bears to the real world. The second puzzle adds to, rather than subtracts from, the fascination of the first.

Herbert Stein
March 22, 1993

Murder
at the
Margin

1

"Now you can see why a parrot could be a passably good economist. Simply teach it to answer 'supply and demand' to every question!" Professor Henry Spearman chuckled as he helped his buxom wife Pidge settle onto the cushioned bench of the power launch. He had just explained to her the price of their taxicab with a supply and demand illustration. The six-dollar fare had taken them and their luggage from the Charlotte Amalie airport to the Red Hook landing on the other side of St. Thomas. Now they were on the last leg of their journey. The boat they had boarded would take them directly to St. John where soon Spearman and his wife would be enjoying dinner at Cinnamon Bay Plantation, the hotel which they had chosen for their holiday.

The flight they had taken that day from New York to the Virgin Islands had been a tiring one, prolonged by a layover in the sultry and crowded San Juan airport. The leisurely boat ride in the fresh sea air was going to be a welcome contrast to the tedium of air travel, Spearman anticipated.

Not that he was opposed to air travel. In fact, that was the way he usually went. In recent years time had become even more valuable to him, and he was often most aware of this when he began to relax. As the boat began its twenty-minute journey across Pillsbury Sound, Spearman thought of how one's expectations often are not realized. When he decided to become a professor, it was partly in the belief that he would have plenty of time to pursue side interests of travel, philately and wide reading—activities that were not options for his father, whose business had required such long hours of attention. But now Henry Spearman's name had become prominent in the economics profession, and it was rare that the hours he put in did not exceed even those that his father had worked. As his reputation grew, the demand for his services grew with it, and his fees for public lectures, guest columns in newspapers, as well as the return on the sales of his books went up in direct proportion. All of this presented him with a paradox. With his increase in income he felt he could afford more leisure activities. At the same time vacations and other leisurely pursuits seemed like luxuries he could ill afford compared to the days when his income was lower. But the paradox was not puzzling to an economist who understood the doctrine of "opportunity cost." For each evening spent enjoying his stamp collection, Spearman gave up the opportunity to work on a lecture, article, or book that would bring him a large monetary return. On balance he decided to choose work over leisure. As his book sales and fees rose, the cost to him of that leisure time went up accordingly. Consequently vacations were rare, his stamp collection generally went unattended, and many extracurricular books remained neglected.

It had always been hard to explain to his family just what it was that took up so much of his time, a problem his father never faced. The elder Spearman had owned a tailor shop. Everyone knew the nature of his work. It was performed in his shop, the product was tangible, and the rewards and disappointments were in the form of profits and losses.

But scholarly research was just the opposite. As an academician, Professor Spearman did much of his work in his head, or unobtrusively hidden away in a library carrel. His work product took the form of books and articles which did not directly pay his salary. That salary was at the top of the Harvard faculty pay scale and was not subject to the vicissitudes of the marketplace as had been his father's earnings.

Spearman also had not expected, when he first took his Ph.D., that preparing lectures for his students would be only a minor part of his duties. Harvard, like any major university, rewarded its faculty for their research, not their classroom performance. Still, Spearman took his teaching duties seriously. His classroom demeanor was not unlike the English tutors of an earlier era who genuinely believed everyone wanted to have their thought processes clarified or corrected. Spearman's impish probing had made him at once the delight and the dread of his students. Over the years the short, balding professor had become a familiar figure to many Harvard students who had been introduced to the rigors of economic thinking in his classes, and the professional accolade he most cherished was the distinguished teaching award conferred upon him by the students of the university. Yes, he thought to himself, his work had taken turns he could not have expected.

About quarter way across the sound, Spearman's reverie was interrupted by a Boston accent. "Professor Spearman, this *is* a pleasant surprise."

Both Professor Spearman and his wife looked up,

quite a way up in fact, to see the gaunt, bearded face of a Harvard colleague, the celebrated theologian Professor Matthew Dyke. Professor Spearman knew Dyke only slightly and feigned pleasure at seeing him. But actually he felt only chagrin in encountering another faculty member on what he had promised himself and his wife would be a get-away-from-it-all expedition.

Professor Spearman's expression belied his real sentiments as he said, "Pidge, you remember Professor Dyke, don't you?"

"How nice to see you," she said quietly, but she shared her husband's feelings about the intrusion.

Spearman's dismay at seeing Dyke was more than matched by Dyke's surprise in seeing Spearman. The economist had a reputation for living and breathing his subject matter and this made him an unlikely candidate, Dyke thought, for a Caribbean vacation.

"With all of the world's economic problems, I did not know you economists could take time off for vacations."

"You may not have heard," Professor Spearman smiled, "that we economists have just met and conveniently decided that the world's problems are ultimately spiritual and so we have agreed to go out of business. Now it's your turn to go to work."

Dyke laughed heartily as he folded his six-foot-seven frame into the seat across from them. Spearman's retort was characteristic. At the faculty club he was known for being quick on the draw. But in point of fact, Professor Spearman was only half jesting, for he had just come from the annual convention of the nation's economists in New York City. As president-elect of the economics association his chief duty had been to plan the meeting and decide all the topics on which scholarly papers would be given. It had been the rigors of this task which led him to the reluctant conclusion that he needed a place to unwind.

Spearman explained all this to Dyke, who in turn pointed out that his visit to the Virgin Islands was prompted by both business and pleasure. He hoped that amidst the beauty of the famed resort at Cinnamon Bay there would be an opportunity to apply the concept of "contextual morality," of which he was a leading exponent. Recent racial disturbances in the islands had persuaded Dyke that his ethical method might find some useful illustrations for a book he planned to write on race and morality.

Professor Dyke's first book, *The Case for a New Morality*, had caused a stir when it first appeared because its conclusions seemed controversial coming from a seminary professor. Indeed the book had become a best-seller, its popularity stemming from the clever incorporation of the scholarly language of theology with the *au courant* language of the youth culture. This combination had proved to have great appeal. But Spearman knew that Dyke's older colleagues in the divinity school considered him a pop theologian.

As Dyke began to expostulate on the research he planned to do, Spearman's hopes for a restful boat trip across Pillsbury Sound began to sink. He was therefore relieved when a steward announced that iced tea would be available during the voyage for one dollar a glass. Professor Spearman made one of those rapid, almost unconscious computations that was second nature to most people but in reality hid a complex series of intermediate steps. With eyebrows raised above his broad spectacles, he examined the tray of tall coolers, each glass garnished with a wedge of fresh lime.

"I'll have a glass," Spearman said. Pidge joined him.

The ratiocination that had led Spearman to this deceptively simple decision to buy a glass of tea had actually involved the following lightning calculation: the probable satisfaction expected from the glass of iced tea being offered exceeded the pleasure from any alternative purchase at that price.

Until Spearman had noticed the lime accompanying the tea, he had been on the margin: he placed the same value on a dollar as he did on a glass of iced tea served without lime. It was the wedge of lime that tipped the scale in favor of purchase.

The man on the street could take such processes for granted and go on to other concerns. The psychologist might pause to notice these mental operations and remark upon the wonder of the human brain. But only the economist could claim to practice a science constructed almost entirely on the premise of such reasoning. Spearman still remembered the excitement he felt when, while a graduate student at Columbia, he discovered the quotation from Alfred North Whitehead which he had been quoting to his students ever since: "Civilization advances by extending the number of important operations which we can perform without thinking about them." The fledgling economist had found satisfaction in the image this gave him of a highly advanced civilization of consumers and producers, the domain of the economist.

They settled back with their tea and Professor Dyke resumed his monologue. At this point Spearman did not even pretend interest in the conversation. He preferred to devote his attention to the scenery: the cays, the sky, the water brought together into a scene of such unreal beauty it was unexpectedly similar to one of those amateurish landscapes done by beginning artists. At times like this Spearman was relieved at the presence of his wife Pidge. One of the benefits of his marriage was her ability to hold up their end of a conversation in which he had lost interest. She had been raised in a professor's home, and pleasantries of the type that she exchanged with Dyke were second nature to her. As Spearman surveyed the tropical vista, over the drone of the boat he could hear his wife's 'How interestings' and 'You don't says' interjected at appropriate moments to fuel Dyke's monologue.

The boat neared the hotel's dock. Conversation began to trail off as the passengers anticipated the transition from the harried pace of travel to the pleasant role of guest at one of the world's great hotels. The captain of the trawler skillfully edged his craft alongside the pier while one of the crew tossed lines to a waiting youth who secured the boat. An aluminum gangplank was glided to the dock and a perky attendant, carrying a clipboard, cheerfully came aboard to greet the guests.

She introduced herself, expressed a welcome to Cinnamon Bay, and read a list of the expected arrivals. Each of the eight passengers on the boat, including the Spearmans and Dyke, were quickly matched with entries on the list, and Spearman made an admiring mental note of the hotel's efficiency. He knew that even seasoned travelers breathed a sigh of relief upon learning that they were expected at their destination and their reservations were in order. After helping his wife down the gangplank, Spearman walked with her towards the registration desk along with some of the other arriving guests.

Professor Dyke stayed behind momentarily to chat with the boat's steward but called out to his Harvard colleague, "I hope you find the peaceful interlude you came for."

"He will," replied the economist's spouse, "I'll see to that."

2

CINNAMON BAY PLANTATION had long been considered by hotel connoisseurs to be one of the world's finest. It was situated on the site of an old sugar plantation, the ruins of which still stood on a hillside overlooking the property. The hotel's several hundred acres included carefully landscaped grounds and gardens as well as hiking trails through dense natural foliage overlooking spectacular views of St. John and the neighboring cays.

By the time the Spearmans had registered and been taken to their cottage, it was late afternoon, and so they had only a small taste of this beauty on the first day of their visit. But this was no great disappointment. It was enough of a delight to them to be able to change out of their flagging travel clothes, be refreshed by a cool shower, and realize that the journey was indeed safely completed. After unpacking their luggage the Spearmans dressed for dinner and left their cottage in the direction of the hotel's cocktail lounge.

The cocktail hour at Cinnamon Bay took place on a veranda overlooking the Sir Francis Drake Channel. At sunset the light reflected off the sails of passing sloops and ketches, and the breezes carried not only the salt air but also the aroma of gardenias and lime blossoms.

"Red sails in the sunset and all that," Professor Dyke tooted when he saw the Spearmans on the veranda enjoying the view. Everyone has met persons who seem unimpressed by even matchless scenes of natural beauty. Dyke was one of these. Not that he was accustomed to this environment. His father had been the pastor of a Moravian church in southern Illinois, and Dyke's upbringing was far from cosmopolitan. The role of super-sophisticate which he now played so well was one he began to assume only after he entered graduate school.

"I suggest the planter's punch," Dyke went on, "it's my favorite. They make it with three different rums and top it with nutmeg."

"Sounds interesting," Spearman responded, "but before I take your suggestion I'd like to see the alternatives."

Pidge, who had found Dyke's proposal appealing, knew that her husband's request to see the bar menu was prompted by more than a desire to examine the range of choice. Her husband also needed to know the various prices attached to each drink before he could make that choice which would yield the highest satisfaction.

"I'll have a piña colada," Spearman told a waiter.

During the cocktail hour Professor Spearman amused himself by observing people's market behavior. What made this endeavor particularly interesting for an economist was the hotel's method of pricing its cocktails: from five to six (the so-called hospitality hour) all drinks were half price; after six o'clock the drinks returned to full fare.

When the waiter returned with their drinks, Henry Spearman signed the chit. Turning back to his wife he remarked, "One of the things I hope to do while we're here is come early for the hospitality hour. I'd be interested to observe how the lower prices affect the rate at which people consume their cocktails. It's a wonderful opportunity to watch the law of demand—the lower the price, the greater the quantity consumed."

Pidge, who had yet to enjoy instruction in elementary economic principles, admonished him. "I thought this was to be a vacation from economics." But she knew her reprimand was fruitless, for her husband was already preoccupied in observing his fellow guests. Mrs. Spearman was used to this. She recalled that even on their first dates, when Henry was still an undergraduate, he could ignore her for much of the evening, so absorbed was he in watching the economic behavior of others. Her husband was even then regularly developing new applications of economic theory for the most commonplace activities, events which to Pidge seemed ordinary but which to her husband represented challenging puzzles. When he would expectantly propose these theories to see her reaction, she would usually miss the significance of his discovery. But instead of presenting a matrimonial impediment, Pidge's economic innocence was a source of amusement to both of them.

Tonight Spearman was wondering how much greater would be Professor Dyke's consumption of planter's punch at the cut-rate price. For even at the full price, he had purchased three during the short time Spearman had observed him.

The professor's musings were interrupted by Dyke's sudden question, "By the way, have you heard the bad news?"

"What news?" Pidge asked. "Is the weather turning bad?"

"No, I mean a real tragedy. I read in today's *Times* that Justice Foote is coming to Cinnamon Bay." Like most Eastern academics Professor Dyke never missed the *New York Times*.

"And that disturbs you?" asked Spearman.

"Of course it does," Dyke replied. "There is no greater evil in America than the influence that man has had on the judiciary. And the audacity of it all." Dyke was obviously agitated, and his words spilled out with great rapidity. "As you know he just resigned from the Court. And the *Times* reported that as his last official act he wrote the majority decision in a case allowing a bigoted shopkeeper to refuse to serve someone solely on the basis of race. Now he's coming here where he will be waited on by the very class of people he is oppressing."

Foote was a former senator from a midwestern state who made his reputation in the Senate for articulate opposition to the trend of more liberal civil rights legislation of the previous decade. But it was his championing of the law-and-order issue that had brought him into national prominence. During a time of great social upheaval, the President of the United States found himself under strong pressure to appoint Foote to the Supreme Court. In four short years Foote had made his opinions the majority view. This he accomplished through an adroit combination of charismatic lectures, a canny understanding of the press, a persuasive, somewhat journalistic writing style (which contrasted with the more stilted legalese of his colleagues) and, some suspected, a bullying manner which cowed two of his more retiring brethren on the Court. When he surprisingly announced his resignation from the Supreme Court some weeks ago the speculation in the press was that he wanted to plan a campaign for the Presidency. Foote had done nothing to quash the rumors.

As Dyke enumerated the failings of Curtis Foote, Spearman shifted restlessly in his chair. He was mildly uneasy whenever anyone espoused what he considered to be a devil theory of history. His economic training had impressed upon him that social reality was much more complex and impersonal than that. But he was saved from further discussion on this point by a tug on his sleeve.

"I'm famished," his wife said. "Let's go to dinner."

The meals at Cinnamon Bay took place in a dining area adjacent to Cinnamon Beach, a short bus ride from the cocktail veranda. One entered from the east through a large double-door portal, the open doors being slung on wrought iron hinges which dated from the plantation days. Covered by a curving roof, two of its sides were completely open, allowing guests exposure to the vistas and the sea breezes. In the event of a blowing rainstorm from the west or north, the waiters would move sliding glass doors into protective positions until the storm had passed. The fourth side, to the south, opened into the hotel's kitchen.

The Spearmans were ushered to their table by the hotel's maitre d'. Professor Spearman picked up the menu that was on his plate and nodded appreciatively. "I had forgotten that dinner was seven courses."

"If we're going to take advantage of all this, we'll need a lot of exercise," his wife added.

"Splendid, just what I wanted." For he had already decided to snorkel and hike extensively. He then wrote out their order on the form and handed it to the waiter, who began to read, half to himself, "Let's see now, you're

having artichoke hearts, the rum and plum soup, plantation salad, dolphin, endives, sherbet, and Camembert."
Mrs. Spearman had the same with one exception. She
chose the cock-a-leekie soup.

After the waiter left, Spearman looked inquisitively
around the dining room. It was the height of the season,
yet half of the tables were empty.

"Not many people are hungry tonight," his wife
stated.

"I think the turnout is not related to people's hunger.
The occupancy rate at the hotel is quite low. Many people
are afraid to come to the Virgin Islands these days."

"Why is that?" Pidge asked, her eyes again scanning
the dining area.

"Because of the racial disturbances. There has been
some rather nasty business on St. Croix and St. Thomas.
As I understand it, aliens from other Caribbean islands
have been encouraged by radical blacks from the states to
make trouble for tourists and wealthy newcomers. They
have actually gone so far as to murder some tourists on
St. Croix."

"My goodness, I hope we are safe here."

Her husband remarked reassuringly, "Don't worry,
there have been no incidents at Cinnamon Bay." The
waiter than brought their first course and the couple
quickly forgot about the political situation in the islands
while they enjoyed the product of the hotel's excellent
kitchen.

As their dessert was being served, the maitre d'
escorted a woman to a nearby table. She was athletic in
appearance, tall, reasonably attractive, and obviously
lost in her thoughts. From her unusually deep suntan, it

was probable that she had been a guest at the hotel for some time.

"Why would a woman come alone to a place like this?"

"Perhaps she values solitude," Spearman replied to his wife as he began sampling his coconut sherbet. "That's certainly a common preference. 'Splendid isolation' as someone once called it. She might simply like solitude and particularly like it here on St. John."

"All the same, this is an expensive place to be alone," Pidge remarked.

The woman noticed she was being discussed and cast a disapproving glance at the Spearmans. Appropriately chastised, they silently finished their meal and departed the dining area toward the north. There they could catch the minibus which transported the guests from the main hotel to deposit them at the various beaches where the cottages were situated. The Spearmans had been given lodging at Turtle Bay, which was one of seven beaches at the hotel. Each beach was known to regular guests for some particular attribute. "Turtle," as it was nicknamed at the hotel, provided the best shallow water snorkeling of the seven.

To get to Turtle Bay involved a bus trip just short of ten minutes. After getting off the bus, the Spearmans walked the fifty feet to their single-room cottage, part of a complex whose architecture was ingeniously unobtrusive within the tropical setting. They quickly came to appreciate the privacy and the simplicity of their surroundings. Inside there were special touches provided by the management: a fragrant English bath soap, a vase of fresh anthurium blossoms, a complimentary bottle of Cruzan rum, and fresh bath and beach towels twice daily. Because of their cottage's proximity to the beach, the sound of the surf washing against the sand provided a soporific back-drop. And it was a gentle surf because their beach was on a broad, quiet bay which curved like a half moon away from the cottages.

"I still have that woman we saw at dinner on my mind," Pidge Spearman said. The book on which she had been trying to concentrate was placed beside her bed. "Do you think we ought to invite her to join us for dinner some evening? She seemed so tense and all alone."

But Henry Spearman did not hear his wife's suggestion. Already tired from traveling, he had been lulled to sleep by the cool breezes and the mesmerizing sounds of the surf.

3

CELEBRITIES WERE NOTHING NEW to Cinnamon Bay. In
fact, presidents, kings, and movie stars regularly took advantage of the salubrious effects of its atmosphere. Even
so, the arrival of Curtis Foote caused some stirring among
the help and guests, in particular those of the fairer sex.
He was the type the liquor advertisements might picture
as a man of distinction. Lightly graying sideburns framed
a thatch of coal black hair which he wore straight back
from his forehead. His clear dark eyes and square, dimpled
chin gave him the appearance of the young Cary Grant.
Women were attracted to him by his rugged good looks as
well as his mantle of importance.

Curtis Foote's judicial philosophy had a resemblance
to that of Chief Justice Roger B. Taney of an earlier era.
Like Taney, Foote placed great emphasis on the sanctity
of physical and tangible property and had a distrust of
federal government powers that were strong enough to
endanger these rights. Unlike Taney, however, Foote had
not been born into the landed gentry. While his roots
were rural, his parents were of modest circumstances and
it was a mystery to Supreme Court observers precisely how
Foote had come to form his judicial principles.

In a way it was out of character for the Justice to visit

Cinnamon Bay, for his recreational tastes ran more to mountain climbing and kayaking. He had been an Olympic kayaker, though not of medal caliber. His wife, the former Virginia Pettingill (of the Oyster Bay Pettingills), was a petite woman whose feminine elegance belied her brilliance at conversation. She also had a reputation for petulance.

"The person who decorated this lobby must be the same one Thoreau hired to do Walden Pond," said Mrs. Foote vexedly.

"It wasn't *my* idea to come to this place for a vacation," her husband replied.

"*Your* idea of a vacation would have us in the middle of Africa swinging on vines like Tarzan and Jane."

Sometimes Virginia's knife went in and out so fast the Justice was unaware of the cut. But this time he felt the insult, and his face visibly reddened. He knew that to a Pettingill, having been a Supreme Court Justice carried no social standing per se. One could only be born into the status of families like the Pettingills. And unlike many other women, Virginia Pettingill Foote was not impressed by his athletic prowess. Thus her reference to Tarzan grated with particular abrasiveness against him.

"Couldn't we continue this discussion in the privacy of our room?" Curtis Foote said, obviously embarrassed.

"But darling," his wife replied sarcastically, "I thought you always wanted a gallery when you spoke." Perhaps the only person in the world who could give Curtis Foote a feeling of insecurity was his wife.

The row of attached cottages to which the Footes were taken was almost on the beach, separated only by a thatch of sea grapes and tall, graceful coconut palms.

Louvres and screens at each end of the room afforded cross ventilation by the gentle ocean breezes. A ceiling fan reminiscent of those in movies starring Humphrey Bogart and Sidney Greenstreet whirred silently overhead. The suite was furnished in bamboo and wicker and, in keeping with the hotel's reputation for quietude, there was no television or radio in the rooms. The nearest telephone was at the reception desk of the hotel's main lobby.

"I hope you folks enjoy your stay," a steward said as he deposited the Footes and their sizable collection of luggage at their two-room suite. Almost an entire room was needed to house Mrs. Foote's latest acquisitions from her favorite couturiers.

"Are there any good jogging trails around the hotel?" the Justice asked of the young man as he was preparing to leave. The ebony-faced steward, uncertain of the meaning of the term jogging, responded, "There are hiking trails around the plantation, sir."

"Those will probably do," Justice Foote said, already planning ways to satisfy his desire to maintain his physical condition.

The first day he sampled all of these trails and decided that Hawksnest Point best suited his requirement for length and rigor. Hawksnest Point was about three miles long, a winding path that in some places cut through dense brush and forest but in others bordered a rocky ridge falling precipitously to the water. The path meandered along a vertical elevation of about three hundred feet and was punctuated with exotic foliage. An observant hiker could find turpentine, licorice, bamboo, and mahogany trees along the rocky and root-studded way. Most conspicuous of these were the kapoks, whose white bark looked like elephant skin and whose roots, which stretched out in all directions, seemed to be greedily claiming land from other foliage.

Another noteworthy feature of the trail was the so-called blowpipe. This was a natural fault in a tall rock bluff which was just off the path. The wedge-shaped fault was about three feet across and looked as though it was gouged out of the cliff itself. The craggy formation in the rock extended down to and below the water, and during high seas the water crashed into the fault and forced air up the pipe, causing an eerie *shooshing* sound to echo from the formation.

The Justice's clocklike regimen of jogging this trail in both the early morning and late afternoon became the subject of much conversation and interest, and it was not uncommon for a few of the guests to wait at the end of the way for his appearance.

In places the trail was so narrow that users had to proceed single file along it. It was at such a place that the jogging Justice once encountered Professor Spearman on a morning stroll. The professor stepped aside to allow the more rapidly moving judge to pass.

"Thank you," said the Justice, showing some exertion.

Since jogging was not, as Spearman himself might have put it, an argument in his own utility function (that is, something conducive to his happiness), he began to reflect on the diverse tastes of the consuming public. He thought to himself that anyone who travels so fast along this trail would miss the natural phenomena along the way and suspected that the Justice had not even seen the kapok trees or the blowpipe.

But in this belief Professor Spearman was mistaken. In Washington, Justice Foote's personal secretary had been instructed to keep a detailed record of the daily activities of her employer. Every appointment, every telephone call, and how Foote's time was divided on Court matters were logged with meticulous attention. To have recorded the daily events of one's occupation was a customary practice for prominent public figures and the order this brought into one's life appealed to Justice Foote. He carried the practice so far as to record even encounters and observations when vacationing. His powers of observation were thereby sharpened well above the average. As it was, the kapok trees, the blowpipe, and much more did not go unnoticed. Even his chance encounter with the short, balding man on the trail would be recorded in his log that evening.

"Got everything down, darling? I just know that future generations will be in your debt for having provided them with a record of what you did today."

Whenever Virginia Pettingill Foote saw her husband making entries in his log, she could not let the occasion pass without comment. She considered this activity another manifestation of her husband's not inconsiderable ego. Mrs. Foote was watching the reflection of her husband in her mirror. She was seated before the vanity, her arms moving gracefully as she first brushed her long auburn hair and then applied a turtle oil night cream.

Justice Foote ignored her comment and kept writing. When his wife was in one of these moods he knew it was best to stay out of her way. But she persisted. She ceased her facial and turned, facing the Justice directly. "Until I married you, I thought only teenage girls kept diaries."

Curtis Foote was not amused. He finished the entries, snapped his book shut, and walked to his bed. "If you think I am going to play one of your Virginia Woolf games tonight, you're sorely mistaken." Foote sat down on his bed and removed his slippers. His wife's petulance always wearied him. He watched her in silence as she carefully completed her beauty routine.

Virginia Pettingill Foote was a woman of mercurial moods. "Good night, love," she said sweetly as she slipped beneath the covers of her bed. Justice Foote sighed, lay back on his pillow, and clicked off the light.

In other cottages at the hotel the routine was different. For example, Mrs. Felicia Doakes of cottage twelve found it increasingly difficult to sleep with the passing years and spent a good part of the night reading. "I'm not as young as I used to be," she thought. Her legs ached from the long periods of standing on the concrete dock that served the town of Cruz Bay. "I really ought not to go there any more," she said to herself. "It's not good for my health. But," she sighed, "there's nothing I can do about it."

By design and not by chance was she in cottage twelve. On her first visit to the islands she had been upset when the management inadvertently assigned her to cottage thirteen, not knowing she had triskaidekaphobia. This fear of the number thirteen she had had as long as she could remember and she tried to avoid any contact with what were to her mind these unlucky digits.

As she read she listened for the sound of the minibus. So precisely was the schedule kept that Mrs. Doakes could rely on the comings and goings of the buses to toll the quarter hours for her. Soon she knew it was a few minutes past midnight, for she could hear the last bus for Turtle Bay arriving at the bus pause.

Not only the vehicles were punctual. Her cousin, General Hudson T. Decker (Ret.), could always be counted upon to disembark from the midnight bus. Now she heard his footsteps heading toward his cottage. He always insisted on number thirteen, claiming it had the most desirable location. She suspected, however, that the General chose thirteen out of spite.

4

GENERAL DECKER, so it was said by the help, was a troublesome man. He always wanted things just so and woe betide the waiter who brought him eggs boiled a few seconds longer or shorter than he had specified. As a general he had become accustomed to having his orders followed, and he expected no less meticulous attention from those who now served him in civilian life.

For Decker breakfast was a major production. His table was situated in the east corner of the dining room because there, he maintained, the lighting was best. This assisted him in scrutinizing each item of his fare. His punctual arrival at nine a.m. was always preceded a few moments before by the scurrying of the waiters, the captain and the maitre d'. To forewarn the chef, a member of the kitchen staff began to watch for the General's arrival at this time so his three-minute eggs could be placed before him almost as he sat down.

"How are you this morning, General Decker?" Duane, one of the dining room captains, inquired solicitously.

"You should be more concerned with how your waiters are. Yesterday Vernon brought my toast too light and my bacon too dark. Not only that, there was no ashtray on my table."

"We'll try to do better today, sir," Duane replied. Decker made no response as he seated himself.

What then ensued was a minor farce. His standing order of eggs was brought to him immediately. But before eating these he placed the rest of his order, all of which he wanted brought to the table at one time. Eventually spread out before him for his approval were two different fruit juices, a cold cereal with bananas, bacon, toast, and skim milk. When all this had arrived, Vernon stood back to await the General's inspection. On the first try the food seldom passed muster.

In a basso voice he announced, "The papaya juice is too chilled. Take it back. And wait, you might as well return the pineapple juice as well. It's obviously not fresh. Tell the chef I want the juice of a freshly crushed pineapple."

By the time the waiter returned with the juice replacements, the General had decided that the kitchen had done no better with the cold cereal since the bananas were irremediably deficient. The General had to work to suppress his temper when confronted with mushy bananas.

"You'd think in the Caribbean one could get a decent banana. Look at the soft spots on this one."

Without argument, the waiter retrieved the offending bowl and hurried to the kitchen. While he was away the General did a remarkable thing. He slowly and carefully lifted each strip of bacon in his fingertips and held it up to the light for his examination. It was his belief that bacon should not be overdone, as tested by its translucency. Opaqueness was grounds for rejection.

The toast ceremony was not as elaborate. The issue here was one of color. The chef had to delineate the fine lines the General drew among brown, dark brown, and burnt. Along this spectrum only dark brown was acceptable.

The chief criterion attached to the final item was simply freshness. The General knew that skim milk was ordered infrequently in any restaurant. Only a modest inventory was kept for these occasional demands. For Decker skim milk that had been on hand more than thirty-six hours was unacceptable and he often argued, the waiter's claims to the contrary, that the milk was stale. Taste was the test.

The serving of the milk could not help but attract notice. The waiter assumed the posture of a sommelier. An amount of milk just sufficient to cover the bottom of a glass was poured. The waiter then stood back while Decker held the glass up, rotating it carefully to catch the light. Slowly he brought the glass to his lips. He sipped a few drops, caught them on the tip of his tongue, and then allowed them to roll back towards his palate. All of the time his eyes were closed as if in deep contemplation while he savored the liquid. Then he swallowed. Only if he looked at the waiter and nodded was it permissible to fill his glass.

Once satisfied that his order was filled to his precise specifications, General Decker sat back and considered his breakfast. Still he did not begin to eat. There was a final ritual. Working with both hands, he moved each dish and glass, pushing and pulling them into alternative locations.

To someone at the next table, these incantations might appear incomprehensible. But in Decker's imagination his breakfast table was transformed into a battle-field. Each course became a regiment strategically placed to engage the enemy. The meal could not be consummated until these maneuvers were completed. At that time the intense expression left his face, and his whole frame relaxed. He consumed his breakfast in a leisurely fashion.

As might be expected, Decker's performance received mixed notices from the other guests. Some dismissed him as a mere *poseur*. But to others, like Mr. Jay Pruitt, of the Pruitt mining fortune, he was a man to be impressed by and to impress. The General's company was solicited at every opportunity by Pruitt, whose personal insecurity had already resulted in two nervous breakdowns and had led possibly (though there was some mystery surrounding the circumstances) to the suicide of his first wife. With his new wife in tow, Pruitt hoped that being in the General's commanding presence would enhance the confident image that he sought to convey to his bride and others. But the General did not cooperate.

"Duane, could we detour past General Decker's table on the way to our own so that I may have a few words with him," Pruitt said. Pruitt, who had the carriage of a dance instructor, was escorted by the obliging captain to Decker's table.

"General, I have something that will interest you. Snorkeling this morning I encountered a *prionace glauca*, that is a barracuda, off the reef near Scott Beach. I was reminded of the billions of dollars the Coast Guard spent in studying the barracuda in order to learn how to make a submarine move quickly from a stationary position. You may have known the man in charge of this project. He is a personal friend of mine, Admiral Norden."

General Decker did not suffer fools gladly. Under the best of circumstances he did not like to be interrupted during his morning repast. And especially did he resent such intrusions by sycophants he considered ignorant.

"Pruitt," he said, his resonant voice carrying through much of the dining room, "you are an inconsequential person, but I cannot let such balderdash go uncorrected. What you encountered was the *sphyraena barracuda*. It was the Navy that studied this fish. The amount spent on the project was six million and its purpose was to learn not how the barracuda moves, which has long been known, but how it hovers. Admiral Templeton headed up the project and he has been dead for some time. Getting one's facts straight is essential."

Casting his eyes upon Mrs. Pruitt he added, "Young lady, it was the constant flow of such gibberish that drove your predecessor to suicide. Wasn't that it, Pruitt?" he asked, looking back.

Pruitt's face reddened as he grabbed his wife by the arm and turned sharply away. This was not the first time he had been humiliated by Decker. The General had on earlier occasions embarrassed him before the other guests. But this was the first time Decker had done so in the presence of Pruitt's bride and had the affrontery to suggest that it was Pruitt's inadequacies that caused the death of his first wife.

"I think he is a perfectly horrid man, Jay. I don't see why you always try to make conversation with him." But Pruitt did not hear his wife's words. He was brooding over the General's remarks and fantasizing how the General might receive his comeuppance.

With rubber beaters the members of the steel band pounded out the strains of "You Cannot Get" on their gaily colored pans. A single performer played two or three oil drums at a time. The band's repertoire ranged from slow-moving simple folk tunes to fast and breezy arrangements that many of the guests at the hotel enjoyed dancing to.

"We going play 'Yellow Bird' tonight. We play now for you," announced the leader of the group. The band at the hotel that night, the Raiders, had a reputation for being one of the best steel bands in the Virgin Islands. Each night it played at one of the various hotels in the area and appeared at Cinnamon Bay three times a week. Its leader, a young black named Ricky LeMans, was proud of his band and its reputation. He himself insisted on making the instruments of his orchestra, and he was a skilled craftsman who took pride in his work. LeMans had perfected the process of cutting off the bung end of a steel container to leave the drum the required depth. He knew just how to hammer the flat surface of the remaining portion of the oil drum into a concave surface and to use a chisel to groove out the notes. The bandleader preferred to play the treble—or ping pong pan as it was called. It was by far the most versatile of the pans.

On this particular evening, Professor and Mrs. Spearman were enjoying the mellow calypso tunes as LeMans's Raiders staged an unusually gay and lively show. Dinner was over, and many of the guests had moved from their tables in the dining area to the adjacent nightclub terrace. Seated with the Spearmans was Mrs. Felicia Doakes of cottage twelve, whom Pidge had befriended on the beach that morning. Mrs. Doakes had shared with Mrs. Spearman some of her recipes for Island cuisine that were going into a cookbook she was currently assembling. Pidge thought it would be nice to invite Mrs. Doakes to join them for the evening.

"Why, Dr. Spearman, I've never even thought why my last cookbook was priced at fourteen dollars. To me that just seemed like a fair price," the author exclaimed, bringing herself more upright.

"But weren't you trying to maximize the income from your book?" the professor asked.

Mrs. Doakes looked taken aback. After all, she never thought of herself as a businesswoman. Writing cookbooks was a hobby, though she did publish them.

"But what if your price had been sixteen dollars?" Spearman pursued.

"That's too high. People aren't accustomed to paying that much for a cookbook. I doubt if I could sell many at that price."

"Why don't you lower your price to twelve dollars then?" He was testing her out.

"As an economist you must know how expensive it is to publish a book these days. And I always insist on color prints and the best paper," she pointed out, a hint of defensiveness in her voice.

"So in other words, Mrs. Doakes, at twelve dollars the price would be below cost and you could not afford to supply the books people would want at that price. At sixteen dollars you could not sell the books you would be willing to supply." By now Spearman was gesturing avidly. "I would say you are a better businesswoman than you imagine or let on. You may think fourteen dollars to be a fair price, but I would add that it is also the most profitable price."

His point made, the short professor sat back in his chair. He knew from past experience with businesspeople their reluctance to claim the motive of profit maximization and was not surprised at Mrs. Doake's hesitancy in this regard. Whenever businessmen argued they did not try to maximize their profits, Spearman assured himself of the theory's validity in the manner which he had used on Mrs. Doakes.

"That's enough economics, Henry," Pidge protested, "I want to hear more of the music." The three of them relaxed and settled back to enjoy the Raiders.

After a short time Mrs. Spearman said: "I don't see why the hotel would hire a band whose leader is known to be a radical." This was murmured half to herself, but her husband took advantage of the opportunity.

"I'm sure the management has its reasons. The hotel is a profit maximizing enterprise. For the amount of money assigned to entertainment, I suspect this is the best orchestra the hotel could obtain for the price. Sometimes an institution concerned only with making profits would consider what its employees did on their off hours as irrelevant."

Mrs. Spearman lapsed into silence and watched the leader of the band perform. Perhaps she was not so much a believer in profit maximizing as her husband, for she found it appropriate to be concerned about what people like LeMans did during his off hours. But this thought, like most of her musings on economics, soon left her, for she was pleasantly distracted by the enchanting, gentle beat of the music.

"I am amazed at the different sounds they can get from some old oil drums," Mrs. Doakes exclaimed, after listening to several numbers.

"What you are hearing now does not begin to exhaust the versatility of the steel band," Professor Spearman replied. "Serious compositions have been written for their use, you know. Indeed, Rodney Dalton of Harvard's music department wrote a concerto for a steel orchestra which was performed during the university's Pan-American festival."

But Felicia Doakes wasn't listening. For her cousin, General Decker, had entered the terrace, and she was disturbed by his presence. "Would you excuse me please?" she said, standing up and retrieving her handbag. "I want to catch the nine o'clock bus back to Turtle Bay and retire early. I must be in Cruz Bay in the morning."

On her way out she passed her cousin. Words were exchanged, which the Spearmans could not overhear, but the economist noticed she left in a huff. The Spearmans remained behind to enjoy their evening.

The final bus to Turtle Bay left the hotel just before midnight. The open-air vehicle was full, and its motor had to strain to pull its heavy load up Sugar Mill Hill on its way to the various beaches. Professor Spearman was seated with his wife toward the front. He tried to watch the passing scene but could only make out vague shadows and dark shapes. Even with a bright moon the nights re-mained dark in the tropics. It was hard to make out the faces of their fellow passengers. Pidge was surprised to feel a slight chill in the air and moved closer to her husband.

In cottage twelve Felicia Doakes was lying awake lis-tening. She knew from the by-now-familiar sounds that the last bus had arrived. She listened for the distinctive footsteps of her cousin. But tonight she heard none. For a lone figure remained on the last seat of the bus after everyone else had disembarked.

When the driver's flashlight shined on the slouching figure, its beam revealed the features of a heavy-set man, his head slouched against his chest. General Hudson T. Decker could not be stirred. The "troublesome man" was dead.

5

THE SUN CAN BE ESPECIALLY HAZARDOUS for bald-headed men. The Virgin Island sun even more so. For this reason Henry Spearman emerged from his cottage wearing a visored golf cap and proceeded in the direction of the beach. The early morning sun was already far more intense than the noonday sun of New England. A newcomer to the hotel had to be especially careful to avoid a painful burn and guests were cautioned to take only a little sun their first day out.

Spearman was determined to have a tan when he returned to Boston. But before settling into that serious business, he wanted to try the snorkeling at Turtle Bay, which he understood to be superb. Donning his snorkel and mask, which his children had given him for the vacation, he waded into the water at the reef end of the bay. After getting used to the cooler temperature, he craned his head into the water and noticed a variety of fish feeding near the coral reefs. A school of palometa, their gills frozen into the semblance of a perpetual smile, swam by his face mask. Deciding this was the place to dive, he submerged himself and entered another world.

Gliding almost effortlessly through the cool and buoyant water, Spearman first encountered three French grunts that seemed to be begging for food. He was sorry he had not brought a breakfast roll from the dining hall. As he circled some elkhorn coral, he watched foureye butterfly fish which, like an old Studebaker, appeared as though either end could be the front.

Spearman moved away from the reef. He swam for a short while and then, having determined that he had reached the point of negative returns in his snorkeling, headed for shore. Dripping wet, he emerged from the water. The sand felt warmly agreeable beneath his feet as he headed for a nearby chaise longue.

Beach chairs never seem to be optimally notched, the economist thought to himself, as he tried to calibrate this particular one to what he considered the ideal angle to the sun. The chair's back was either too high or too low. He finally decided on the more upright position and settled himself in. Around him the white coral sand sparkled like a Tiffany window. And facing him the colors of the water were variegated and brilliant—at the shore's edge, the sea was crystal clear, then a light aquamarine tint emerged, becoming a deeper and deeper blue until, at the horizon, the water appeared to be blue-black ink.

As he relaxed, he reflected how university politics, so seriously taken at Harvard, seemed inconsequential from the island of St. John. His own department sustained a running feud between those who conceived of economic analysis as essentially a logical exercise and those who thought it was an empirical science. He liked to think his own work bridged both views but the theorists considered him a member of their camp. Spearman did not argue the point. He had always been able to keep his enthusiasm for such methodological disputes under control. As university problems drifted from his mind, his attention was brought back to the beach when a Frisbee skimmed under his chaise longue. Spearman's arms were too short to reach under the chair from a sitting position so he got up to fetch the disc.

"Thank you!" a young man cried out from a few yards down the beach.

"Sorry to trouble you," his female companion added as Spearman tried unsuccessfully to pitch the Frisbee in their direction. The couple struck him as being not much older than his graduate students and, from their tans, he assumed they had been here almost a week.

"I hope we did not disturb you," the woman said as they both strolled over to retrieve the Frisbee. "This belongs to our two boys. We both could use throwing lessons from them."

"Judging from my efforts, all three of us would benefit," Spearman replied, meeting the couple halfway. "Perhaps we could hire them to give us instructions," he added, smiling.

"Too late for that now," the woman said, "They left Cinnamon yesterday to stay with their grandparents. We were here as a family all last week. This week is going to be our real vacation, with the boys off in Michigan. By the way, we're the Clarks, Doug and Judy."

"I'm Henry Spearman; it's a pleasure I'm sure."

Spearman had almost forgotten how clean-cut some young people still were. Long hair and old clothes had become almost a uniform with his students at Harvard. The Clarks were cut from a different cloth. Wearing seersucker bermudas and a red Chemise Lacoste, Mr. Clark, with his neatly cropped hair and square-jawed features, looked like Princeton '62. Mrs. Clark, in a red print sun dress, conveyed a wholesome Midwestern image.

Judy was a talkative girl, and it was not long before the Harvard professor knew she was from Michigan, that her father was in the automobile industry, that her mother gardened extensively, and that she had met Doug at college. "I know it sounds banal, Mr. Spearman, but it was love at first sight."

On the other hand, Doug was more reticent to speak. Spearman learned that he was a medical doctor, but beyond that the young man offered little detail. Judy allowed as how her husband had two brothers but the younger had been killed in Vietnam. His family was from Kalamazoo. They had been occupying their time during this vacation with beach activities during the day and, somewhat to Spearman's surprise, nightclubbing in the evening. Judy indicated that they spent most every evening last week visiting the nightclubs in the nearby town of Cruz Bay.

"I just love to dance, and so does Doug—but not as much as I do." She giggled slightly and acted embarrassed. Spearman thought she looked even younger than her thirty-three years.

"I told Doug that he had his scuba diving during the day and I want to dance during the night and he has been wonderful about it. Of course, that has meant a sitter each night while the children were here. But the places in Cruz Bay are less expensive than that beautiful nightclub in the hotel. Have you been there yet, Professor? We tried it last night."

"Scuba diving in the day against going dancing in the evening—I don't think I would accept those terms.

Sounds like your wife drives a hard bargain," Spearman quipped to the young doctor.

"Not really," Dr. Clark replied, "I became mildly addicted to scuba diving when stationed in Thailand and I'm now certified."

The conversation was interrupted at this juncture by Pidge Spearman, who appeared with a grievously troubled look on her face.

"Henry, I feel such concern for Mrs. Doakes. Her cousin—you remember the man she spoke to as she left the terrace last night—has been found dead."

"Oh poor chap, what was it? His heart?"

"The police don't know it yet, but they suspect he was poisoned."

"You mean food poisoning?"

"I mean that he was *deliberately* poisoned." She paused and swallowed hard.

"Deliber—"

"And there's something else you should know. We were with the man last night when he died."

"With him? Where?"

"They found his body on the last bus to Turtle Bay!"

6

DETECTIVE VINCENT knew that Walter Wyatt, the manager of Cinnamon Bay Plantation, resented his presence. Tourism in the Islands was already in a state of decline. But Vincent had a job to do, and the thin, balding police officer seemed determined to do it. His eyes stared resolutely into Wyatt's as he said, "I am aware that your guests haven't come to Cinnamon to be interrogated. But a murder has been committed here. And I have to assume that the murderer either was or still is at your hotel."

"I understand that, but I trust you will be as discreet as possible. The occupancy rate is only seventy percent right now. If you drive away many of the guests, and stir up things so much that others won't come, the owners might decide to close the place down."

"Neither of us wants that to happen. But I have a crime to solve. And that will involve making inquiries of those who were near General Decker the night of his death. I would like you to announce to your staff that some of them can expect to be questioned as well. Now if you will excuse me." Inspector Vincent turned on his heel and briskly strode from the manager's office.

Franklin Vincent was the lone detective on the small police force at Cruz Bay. Murders were not in his normal line of work. He was more often to be found investigating the theft of an outboard motor or the disappearance of a goat. Wearing leather sandals with dark knee socks and bermudas, Vincent certainly did not resemble any member of a big city's homicide squad. As he left Wyatt's office, he was thinking of how much he wanted to solve this crime without the assistance of any of his counterparts on the islands of St. Thomas and St. Croix. While these police officers were from more urban areas and had more experience with crimes of violence, Vincent resented the air of superiority he sensed they had towards him. Only as a last recourse would he seek aid from anyone.

Still, he began by asking himself what Inspector Aberfield of the Charlotte Amalie police force would do. Placing himself in the role of Aberfield, he decided first to nose around the hotel and see if anyone spotted something unusual the night of the murder.

When he arrived at the hotel at four o'clock in the afternoon, he found a number of the hotel's guests gathered at tables near the cocktail terrace for hot tea and cookies. Among them were Henry Spearman and Judy Clark, who, unlike their spouses, enjoyed the afternoon refreshments. Uninvited, Franklin Vincent joined them.

"Afternoon, I'm Inspector Vincent of the Cruz Bay police force. Here is my badge," he said, unfolding his wallet before Professor Spearman and his companion. He sat down to join them, and Spearman offered to get the inspector some tea and cookies.

Vincent hesitated before answering, but he declined the offer. "No thanks." Actually he would have enjoyed some tea and cookies at this time, but he could not imagine Inspector Aberfield having refreshments while conducting a homicide investigation. "This should only take a few moments. I have some questions I want to ask you." Vincent turned to the professor. He quickly learned Spearman's name, his occupation, his home address, and how long he had been at the hotel. When Vincent found out that the professor did not know General Decker, he showed no emotion. But his ears did perk up when Spearman indicated he had seen the General the night of his death.

"How's that?" Vincent asked.

"His cousin, Mrs. Felicia Doakes, was having cocktails with us that evening, and when she left early to return to her room, she exchanged a few words with him."

"Let me get that name," the detective said, reaching into his shirt pocket for a small pad and pencil. "Is she a guest at the hotel?"

"Yes, she is staying near us in cottage twelve at Turtle Bay."

"That puts her right next to the deceased. She must be pretty broken up about this—I mean, his being her cousin and all."

Spearman thought awhile before answering. "Mrs. Doakes does not strike me as a sentimental woman. I think you would be able to interview her without causing her undue distress."

"Is there anything you saw at cocktails last night you think I ought to know?" Vincent asked, holding his pad and pencil at the ready. Spearman remembered the rather curt meeting Mrs. Doakes had had with General Decker that night before she left the terrace. But he decided against mentioning it to the detective since it was probably unimportant and he did not want to arouse unwarranted suspicion in the detective's mind.

"It turns out, although I did not know it at the time, that my wife and I were on the minibus with General Decker at the time of his death. But in the darkness neither of us saw the man and I did not learn of his death until the next day." The detective looked at Spearman uncertainly and wrote on his pad.

Turning to Judy Clark, the detective made the same preliminary inquiries. "Were you and your husband at the hotel that evening, Mrs. Clark?"

"Why, yes sir," she replied, "in fact, we both spent the evening at the hotel's lounge dancing to the steel band. I have been quite upset by the whole matter ever since. It was the first night we had ever gone dancing here and our table was very close to his." She paused. "We had been warned to be careful the nights we went dancing in Cruz Bay. But we never thought there could be any trouble at a place as high-class as this. All I can say is that I am happy our children went home to my parents just before this happened."

"You and your husband should be careful nightclubbing in Cruz Bay," the inspector said. "Those places can attract a rough crowd." Pausing, he then asked, "How did you happen to be at Cinnamon the night of the murder?"

"Well, because we didn't need to hire a sitter. By that time our children had left, and we decided we could afford to go to a fancier place."

Spearman looked at her curiously as the inspector asked, "Is your husband around? Since he was with you that night, I would like to see him as well. He may have spotted something you didn't."

"He went on a boat this morning to Trunk Bay to do some scuba diving. He should be back soon."

Detective Vincent rose to his feet. "Well, that'll be all—unless you think there is anything else I should know." He began to move to another table.

"Officer," Judy Clark said hesitantly, "I really didn't want to say anything about it, and I'm sure it's not important, but there is one man here I know did not get along with General Decker."

"And who is that?" he inquired, seating himself again.

"I believe his name is Mr. Pruitt. My husband and I saw General Decker put him down rather rudely a few times in front of other guests. Mr. Pruitt seemed terribly sensitive about it."

"What exactly did Decker do?" Vincent asked as he scribbled some notes.

"Why, just this Monday I overheard General Decker upbraid Mr. Pruitt severely for not knowing the difference between crab and lobster. Mr. Pruitt was telling people that one of the platters on the buffet table was stacked with spiny lobster when General Decker announced that Pruitt was all wet, or something to that effect, that in fact the shellfish we were eating was Dungeness crab. Later that evening Decker corrected Mr. Pruitt again during a dispute about the island's history."

"Thank you very much, Mrs. Clark, you have been most helpful. And you too, Dr. Spearman. Thank you." Professor Spearman seemed roused from his thoughts.

"Oh, you're welcome," he said, "I trust you'll find the murderer."

Inspector Vincent rose again to leave. He was soon to discover that Mrs. Clark's observations about Jay Pruitt and the General were quite accurate. More than one guest recounted similar incidents involving the two men.

Franklin Vincent spent the rest of that day and a good part of the next asking questions of other guests, concentrating particularly on those who had met General Decker or who had been present at the cocktail terrace the night of his death. Satisfied that he had all the information he could get from these sources, the detective decided next to focus on that group which he felt most likely to hold the General's murderer: the hotel's help. He had learned from Mr. Wyatt and others that Decker was considered distastefully dictatorial in many of his dealings with the staff. In particular Vincent was interested in Vernon Harbley, who usually had been the General's waiter and had served him the night of his death.

Vernon Harbley was a native of St. John, a tall, handsome bachelor who had chosen not to live in the hotel's accommodations for its help, but instead resided in Cruz Bay. He had been a waiter at the hotel for several months; an examination of his file showed there had been no customer complaints about his work.

Vincent arranged to question the General's waiter in a small anteroom off the dining area. This location afforded the two of them the privacy the detective wanted. He had decided to use a blunter mode of interrogation with the hotel's help, thinking he might catch them off guard or provoke them into a revealing response that would otherwise not be offered.

Yet Vincent knew this tactic could backfire. The hotel's employees were predominantly natives of the Virgin Islands and they harbored the same suspicions and, in some cases, hostility toward the police as many blacks in the continental United States. Moreover, while the hotel's work force was not unionized, there was a solidarity among the help which might lead them to protect each other by refusing to provide information. Vincent was aware of all this as he began his questioning. "Vernon, did you hate General Decker?"

"I didn't like the man—but I didn't hate him enough to kill him if that's what you're getting at," the waiter exclaimed, smoking nervously and looking down at the floor.

"He was cruel to you, wasn't he? Always complaining? Making you take things back and forth to the kitchen? Isn't that why you hated him?"

"I didn't like the way he ordered us around. But I didn't poison him."

The inspector tried to be as insistent in his questioning as he imagined Aberfield would be. At one point he put his finger under Harbley's nose and shook it, continuing to interrogate him in an accusatory tone of voice. "It would have been easy for you to poison him, wouldn't it? You served him food every day. And you were his waiter at the bar that night."

"It would have been easy for many others to have poisoned him as well. What about the woman he was with? Why don't you question her? Is it because she's white?" Vernon Harbley was both angry and frightened. His hands shook and he breathed heavily as he made these last statements to his interrogator.

The detective's attitude became visibly altered: "Woman? What woman? Decker was a bachelor, and I understood he always dined alone." Vincent looked puzzled, but Harbley was insistent.

"He usually dined alone. But that night the General noticed a lady—a lady who usually ate by herself. He gave me his calling card to take to her. There was a note on the back asking her if she would join him at his table for dinner. I took the card over and she accepted."

"Who was this woman, do you know?"

"I don't know her name but I remember her. She is pretty and strong looking. I think Duane said she was from the States. She has been a guest here for some time and I think she's still here. Duane would know her name."

Vincent planned to question the woman and made a note to get her name from the captain. This was the first he had heard about this incident. But he continued to be skeptical of Vernon Harbley. Harbley, like a number of the young waiters who were Virgin Island natives, was associated with the local black power movement and was a known disciple of another man who was high on Inspector Vernon's list of suspects—Ricky LeMans.

7

RICKY LEMANS'S REPUTATION as a versatile musician and as a craftsman had been exceeded only by his growing fame among the islanders as a cunning and resourceful politician. The hotel brought him and his band to entertain the guests knowing full well that LeMans was a black power advocate. Apart from purchasing his musical skills, they also hoped to co-opt the talented young radical. Paying him lucrative fees to entertain the guests, the manager thought, might make LeMans more agreeable to coexistence with the white power structure. Besides, his band was good, one of the best in the islands. The calypso melodies were particularly appreciated at the five o'clock cocktail hour when he appeared on the veranda entertaining the guests before dinner. The music seemed to whet their appetites for the hotel's rum specialties. LeMans played at the hotel three days during the week, receiving one hundred fifty dollars both for the cocktail hour and later after-dinner performances. The sum was considerably higher on Saturday. For on that day the band was hired to conduct an afternoon concert, as well. This event had become popular not only with the hotel's regular guests but also with the gentry of St. John who came to Cinnamon for a leisurely lunch, a dip, and the music. Because the band had to spend the afternoon and evening at the hotel, Cinnamon Bay paid LeMans twice his weeknight fee.

Inspector Vincent knew that if it was the hotel's intention to co-opt LeMans, the result was precisely the opposite. LeMans had come to resent the white race even more after seeing them in the luxury hotel, realizing that the price of one night's lodging was more than the salary of a typical native Virgin Islander for one week. But LeMans continued to play. Financing his political activity was expensive—pamphlets, a radical newsletter, and travel all cost him a great deal of money. So much, in fact, that it was commonly believed that he had an outside source of financial support. Vincent also had observed that LeMans found it convenient to meet other blacks who worked at the hotel, since he could enlist them in his designs to make the tourists feel unwelcome and hurt the white man's business. The murder of General Decker, Vincent surmised, could be part of LeMans's plan to destroy tourism on the islands, and so today he decided to concentrate his efforts on the bandleader.

Inspector Vincent left his office at the police station and ambled over to the square. He had always found it a useful place to get information on stolen items; perhaps today, he thought, he could learn about a murder.

St. John's Square in Cruz Bay was the focal point of the village. Located just east of the public dock, it was an unimposing dirt park with about a dozen benches. It was bordered on two sides by local shops and businesses, by the customs and immigration building on another, with the open side facing the waterfront. At any time of the day indigenous citizens and visitors congregated at St. John's, and it was there that the local grapevine had its roots.

A visit to the town square revealed that life in Cruz

Bay went on at an unhurried pace. Indeed, compared to the activity on St. Thomas, Cruz Bay was a sleepy village. It attracted only a handful of tourists compared to the thousands who jammed the streets of Charlotte Amalie. At the square that day, a number of young people were waiting for a taxi-truck to take them to the National Park campgrounds; some of the village's elderly residents had taken up their usual spots on the benches tacitly reserved for them; and the only commotion of any note was a group congregated at the front of the scuba shop. They had just returned from a dive and were enthusiastically comparing notes. Vincent was disappointed at the absence of any people he would have counted as cronies of LeMans. And the bandleader himself did not make an appearance.

What would Aberfield do now, Vincent wondered, taking out a rumpled handkerchief to mop his brow. He sat down on a bench to think about his next move when his attention was caught by an item on the seat next to him. His eyes registered a disapproving look as he noticed the drawing of the petroglyph at the top and he knew that another copy of the *Raider* had been printed. The *Raider* was a newsletter put out sporadically by Ricky LeMans and circulated among black natives on the island. It was a slick pamphlet done in offset on yellow newsprint and its symbol was a strange and primitive design found carved in some rock formations on the island of St. John:

Although nothing conclusive had been established, some archeologists speculated that the petroglyphs were done by slaves hiding out on the island after the slave rebellion of 1733.

Vincent was familiar with the *Raider*, but he had not yet seen this issue. He picked up the copy and turned immediately to the back page. In each issue this page was devoted to a profile entitled TARGET, which identified some individual considered unsympathetic to the LeMans version of black power tactics. These profiles singled out for vilification wealthy landowners and businessmen on the islands, local politicians, and eminent visitors to the area. The column listed the home address, phone number, names and ages of the subject's children, as well as identifying the schools they attended. While TARGET never contained overt instructions, harassment frequently accompanied the dubious honor of being profiled in the *Raider*.

The expression on his face went from disapproval to consternation when he saw the name General Hudson T. Decker staring at him in bold letters. "So Decker had been the latest target," the detective said, half to himself. Franklin Vincent knew what he would do now. He rose from the bench and walked to the police station. It was time to pay a call on Ricky LeMans.

"Would you give me the keys to one of the jeeps, Milan? I'm going to Ricky LeMans's place to pick him up for questioning." Sergeant Milan Queller handed him the keys to one of the blue and copper jeeps which served as police cars on St. John. "You won't find him at home today," Queller said; "I saw him leave this morning on the ferry to St. Croix."

"Let me know if you see him come back to Cruz Bay. I'll take the keys anyway and drive over to see Mamie LeMans." Vincent started the jeep and drove out Center Line Road in the direction of LeMans's mother's house. As he pressed on the accelerator, the jeep's canvas top flapped in the wind with a staccato rhythm. The speedometer being broken, Vincent had come to judge the jeep's speed by the rapidity of the *tut-tut-tut-tut*.

Mamie LeMans lived in the hills back of Cruz Bay. Her small wooden cottage was ramshackle in appearance and construction. Parts of it had never been painted, and the roof had a noticeable sag at its peak. The house was built on a stilt foundation of cinder blocks and could be approached only by traveling a narrow, steep and rocky drive. Inspector Vincent was wise to take a jeep. As soon as the detective pulled up to the dwelling, he noticed Mamie in the backyard milking a goat. He shooed away the chickens as he walked toward the woman.

"What you want out this way, Mr. Vincent? I got no business for the police. 'Sides, I got to milk this goat 'order to have milk for supper."

"Is Ricky coming for supper tonight, Mamie?"

"Ricky? What you asking about Ricky fo'? He got no business fo' the police." She picked up the bucket of goat's milk and headed for her house. Vincent trailed after her.

"Mamie, I want to ask you a few questions about Ricky. Did he ever mention a General Decker to you?" Mrs. LeMans did not answer. "Does Ricky ever have any meetings out here? Who have you seen him with lately?" Vincent persisted, following her onto the front porch.

"Why would Ricky want to meet here? Place ain't got no screens—they all busted out. And bugs eat you up out here. 'Sides, I don't see Ricky much. He keeps to himself and that band of his. Why you askin' all these questions?"

"Mamie, I've known you for twenty years. And there wasn't a time that you didn't know what Ricky was up to," the detective cajoled.

"That' befo' he met Vernon Harbley."

"Harbley? The waiter over at the Cinnamon Bay?"

Mamie LeMans went inside her house and without hesitation Vincent followed her in. The unmistakable aroma of peanut soup permeated the one-room shack, reminding the detective that he had not eaten since breakfast.

"Mamie, does Ricky hang around with Vernon Harbley? Anybody else?"

"You wan' some peanut soup?" was Mamie's reply.

"Fine, if you have some to spare. But you haven't told me what Vernon and Ricky are up to that keeps Ricky from visiting his old mother as often as he should." Mamie ladled two bowls of soup and placed them on the table, motioning to the police officer to be seated. With a sigh she eased herself onto a chair across from him. Inspector Vincent said grace silently, and the two of them began sipping their soup.

While Inspector Vincent was finishing the bowl, his conversation with Ricky LeMans's mother made it apparent that she was not going to reveal much about her son's recent activities. He smiled as he rose from the table and headed for the door. "You still make excellent peanut soup, Mamie."

Mrs. LeMans sighed. "Ricky use' to like my peanut soup—but he got fancy ideas 'bout food since him and his band play at Cinnamon Bay."

"You can give me Ricky's share of your peanut soup anytime. And if you ever want to tell me something about Ricky that you think I should know, you come down to Cruz Bay. I might be able to keep him out of trouble." Vincent walked out of the house and entered the jeep.

On his return to the police station Franklin Vincent

made a call at the Cruz Bay apothecary. The forensic tox-icologist had found that General Decker died of circula-tory collapse and respiratory failure induced by mepho-barbital, a delayed response poison readily soluble in food or alcoholic drinks. The detective was interested in learn-ing if the pharmacist could report any unusual sales of this particular barbiturate compound, or anything which con-tained it, to Ricky LeMans or someone associated with the bandleader. Receiving a negative reply, he then in-quired as to whether any guests at the Cinnamon Bay Plantation had bought any pharmaceuticals containing this toxin. The druggist carefully checked his records for the past month and came up with nothing. As he left, on an impulse, he bought some yellow ribbon. "Mamie would like this," he thought.

A tattered and faded United States flag hung over the pink cinder block building. A sign above the front door identified the structure:

DEPT. OF PUBLIC SAFETY

POLICE DIV.

CRUZ BAY, ST. JOHN

Henry Spearman hesitated as he examined the sign. He was unaccustomed to visiting police stations, but he decided his information necessitated this call. He opened the door and asked at the desk, "I would like a word with the person who is in charge of the murder investigation at Cinnamon Bay. I believe the man's name is Inspector Vincent." Before the desk sergeant could answer, the door opened again and the officer whom Spearman had met the day before entered.

"Franklin, this man wants to see you about the Decker murder."

Vincent was surprised to see the short, balding gentleman. He recalled that his visitor was a professor who, two days before, could tell him very little about the murder. Vincent was curious and invited Spearman into his office.

Sitting beside a gray metal desk with a broken glass top, Spearman began to explain his presence to the attentive investigator. But he was not long into his narrative before Vincent's face took on an expression of perplexity. "Now let's get this straight, Professor. You think you know who the murderer is based on economic theory?"

"I am sure of it."

Inspector Vincent sat back in his chair, not knowing whether to be irritated or amused. Perhaps the professor was some kind of crackpot. Spearman began to explain his economic reasoning. But Vincent simply stared at him in disbelief. As Spearman approached his incriminating conclusion, Vincent interrupted him, "Well, Professor, I confess I just don't follow all that. And frankly I can't see what this business about economic laws and demand and stuff has to do with murder. I'm afraid I need more than just theories in order to put murderers behind bars."

"But surely on the basis of what I've said you'll want to hear me out so you can investigate my hypothesis further."

"Absolutely not! From what you tell me I can't see as how anyone has broken the law."

Spearman looked up and noticed the set of volumes entitled *Virgin Islands Code Annotated* on a shelf above Vincent's desk. "The laws I deal with in economics are not the laws you deal with in police work. Economic laws cannot be broken."

"Laws that cannot be broken," Vincent said, "are of no interest to me."

"But they should be," Spearman thought. "They should be. And perhaps I shall be able to prove it."

8

THE AROMA OF BAY RUM wafted into the open-air pavilion which served as the nightclub for Cinnamon Bay. The fragrance of tropic gardenias mixed with the expensive perfumes of the guests. Ricky LeMans and his band had already begun to play before the room was filled. Strains of "Marianne" poured forth as the hotel guests drifted in for the evening's entertainment.

Inspector Vincent was at the hotel this evening. He had decided that Aberfield, his counterpart on the force at Charlotte Amalie, would give close and continuing observation to the scene of the crime. And he, Vincent, would do no less. Also, tonight was one of the Raiders' scheduled appearances at the hotel, so he would have a good opportunity to question LeMans and his band members and also keep watch on Vernon Harbley. Meanwhile, the inspector's eyes roamed over the room.

At a table near the center of the pavilion was seated Felicia Doakes and Professor Matthew Dyke. Dyke's flippancy during his interrogation had irritated the inspector, but he could think of no reason to suspect the angular theologian. Still, tonight Dyke was with Mrs. Doakes, whose dislike of Decker had been evident to more than one guest and even to Vincent during his interview with her. It was hard for Vincent to imagine Mrs. Doakes carrying out a murder single-handedly, but a conspiracy could not be ruled out. Dyke and Mrs. Doakes were talking earnestly, their heads close together, and Vincent thought to himself how he would like to know what engaged their attention so much that they seemed oblivious to their surroundings. Perhaps a knowledge of what they were saying would tell him more about the circumstances surrounding the murder than either one had been willing to reveal earlier to the police. Had Vincent been able to overhear the discussion between them, he would have had some difficulty relating its content to his suspicions of a conspiracy. For the conversation at that time was concerning recipes for unusual West Indian cuisine.

Dressed in a very conservatively tailored blue and white seersucker suit and seated by herself directly across the room from Vincent was the athletic-looking woman who had been seen on at least one occasion at General Decker's table. Vincent had learned that her name was Laura Burk. She was the only young unescorted female guest at the hotel, and she had explained her encounter with General Decker as being quite innocent—he had simply invited her to have dinner with him, and she had accepted. He was not all that unattractive, she had added, an older but distinguished gentleman. After dinner that night she had excused herself with a slight headache and returned to her cottage early. Miss Burk claimed she did not learn of the General's death until the next day. Vincent looked at her closely. He believed that headaches were a womanish complaint, but somehow he did not correlate this malady with such an athletic-looking type.

Vincent's attention was then drawn to the entrance, where Henry Spearman and his wife Pidge were being greeted by the maitre d'. The sight of the Spearmans reminded him of that afternoon's nonsensical conversation, and he wondered if Aberfield ever had to deal with characters like the Harvard economist. Vincent hoped he could avoid future encounters with Spearman, whom he had dismissed as a crank.

"Dr. and Mrs. Spearman, won't you join us?" Jay Pruitt's voice called out as the Spearmans were being led to a table.

"Let's do," Pidge said, "I've met Mrs. Pruitt on the beach, and we both share an interest in oriental rugs. And her husband seems to know about all sorts of things." Spearman smiled in response. He did not expect to learn about "all sorts of things," but he accepted the invitation.

"Not afraid to sit with public enemy number one?" Jay Pruitt was relishing his role as a chief suspect in the Decker death. It had given him the attention he seemed to crave, and he even exaggerated his importance by claiming that he was under orders not to leave the hotel.

"The pleasure is all mine. The closest I have ever been previously to public enemy number one is when I encountered his picture at the post office. If you do in fact make the list, I shall someday be delighted to point you out to my friends."

Pruitt leered at Spearman and laughed. Then, abruptly, he inquired, "Do you see that woman dancing over there?" He gestured toward a middle-aged woman wearing a black off-the-shoulder cocktail dress who was dancing with her husband, a man of about fifty in a rather youthful leisure suit. "I tried to get her to dance with me yesterday, and she said she didn't enjoy dancing. But that can't be true. Obviously she likes dancing. Look at the happy expression on her face."

"What she told you may very well be true," Henry Spearman replied. "Probably was, in fact. She and her husband may simply have interdependent utility functions, like so many married couples. That's what economists mean by 'love.'"

"Interdependent what?" Pruitt responded.

"Interdependent utility functions. I'm sure you have one at times. It simply means that the pleasure you get from some of your activities is dependent upon the happiness of another. So for example the lady in question may get utility, or to put it another way, satisfaction, from knowing that her husband has a good time on his vacation. If he enjoys dancing, and she doesn't, she still would gladly dance since her utility in this instance is dependent upon her husband's."

"So now you're explaining even love through economics, Henry? Isn't that going a bit far?" Pidge asked.

"Love, hate, benevolence, malevolence or any emotion which involves others can be subjected to economic analysis. When I say 'I love you,' it means my utility or happiness is intertwined with yours. Of course, the expression would be hard to work into a love song." Henry Spearman seemed pleased with his explanation.

Pamela Pruitt, however, looked bored by the academic exposition on the economics of love and thought it quite inappropriate for cocktail chatter. She changed the subject as soon as an opening in the conversation offered itself. "Jay, I believe that couple likes dancing almost as much as you do," she interjected, nodding in the direction of the dance floor. Her husband and the Spearmans looked up and saw that Mrs. Pruitt had noticed Doug and Judy Clark.

"Those are the Clarks from Michigan," Mrs. Spearman said. "Their cottage adjoins ours on Turtle Bay. And you are right about their loving dancing—or at least *she* does. They recently sent their children back to stay with their grandparents, and Judy told me that, with no need to worry about hiring a sitter, they would really be enjoying the dancing here at the hotel."

Jay Pruitt watched them for awhile and judged, "Well, neither one of them is very good at it. C'mon honey, let's show them how to move to these Caribbean rhythms." As the Pruitts maneuvered to the dance floor, they brushed past Justice and Mrs. Curtis Foote, who were making their way to a table. More than a few heads turned when the Footes arrived—not so much because of the fame of the jurist as because of the always stunning attire of his wife. This evening Virginia Pettingill Foote was wearing an orange silk caftan, her only adornment being a silver chain necklace from which dangled a triangular pendant. A brilliant diamond accented each angle of the ornament, which hung at her waist.

Seating themselves at an empty table near the Spearmans, the Footes came under the watchful gaze of Inspector Vincent. The Cruz Bay detective thought there was no reason to hold the Footes under any suspicion. Although they had been present on the night of Decker's death, Vincent reasoned that Supreme Court justices were unlikely murderers, as was any member of the Pettingill family. Besides, his cursory check of the Footes' background showed no connection with the deceased. It was not the Footes but rather their table that interested Vincent. For they were seated within Vernon Harbley's station. Harbley, Vincent knew, had waited on General

Decker on the night of his murder and had had a myriad of opportunities to administer the lethal poison that caused his death. Moreover, Vincent was aware that the waiter detested the whites he so solicitously served. The chilling thought occurred to the inspector that Justice Foote might be in some danger since the black power movement was likely to consider Foote as an enemy. The inspector made a mental note to warn the former judge that he should be on his guard.

Vincent's attention, along with most everyone else's, for that matter, was then caught by the spectacle on the dance floor. Only one couple remained on the long wooden pallet in front of the band. The other dancers had abandoned their efforts, some out of admiration for the dancing performance they were now witnessing. A good dancer will often step aside for a truly superb one. Others had narrower motives. They either did not want to be shown up in their dancing prowess or, in this case perhaps, they were choosing to avoid physical injury. That possibility was not remote. Jay Pruitt's antics on the dance floor involved periodic leaps in the air with legs extended in a vee shape, his hands stretching out to touch his toes. Upon landing he often dropped into the crouched posture of a Cossack Gopak dancer, his arms folded to his chest, his legs kicking seriatim. His most expansive movement was a nimble backwards somersault, executed impetuously and without warning, from which he always rose to the beat of the music. All the while he clasped a pipe in his mouth, seemingly without effort. During this exhibition his wife had found it prudent to give him center stage while she danced a solitary calypso.

Doug and Judy Clark were one of the couples to leave

the dance floor in response to Pruitt's gyrations. As they returned to the table they had previously occupied, they noticed that it was now engaged by the Footes. "Doug, isn't that our table? It's been taken by the Supreme Court justice and his wife!"

"Shall I tell them that that was our table?" he asked.

"Goodness no, let's find another place." Judy's head began to turn in search of alternatives.

Pidge Spearman, who liked the Clarks very much, noticed their predicament. "Won't you join us over here? These are taken by the Pruitts," she nodded at the two empty chairs, "but there's room at our table." Henry Spearman obligingly rose and fetched two more chairs.

"Quite a display, isn't it?" Pidge Spearman exclaimed.

"You mean Jay Pruitt?" the Clarks replied.

"Yes, I've never seen anyone dance like that before." Mrs. Spearman was used to a more sedate style of dancing, where the partners held one another as they glided across the dance floor. She thought she disapproved of Pruitt's dancing demeanor, but she did not show it as he and his wife returned to the table.

"You know the Clarks, don't you?" Spearman asked.

"Oh, you mean the good doctor over here," Jay Pruitt replied, staring in Douglas Clark's direction.

"Yes," Mrs. Spearman interjected, "Dr. Douglas Clark and his wife Judy."

"We have already met the Pruitts," Dr. Clark said. "The last time we chatted, as I recall, he told me the proper way to administer an injection."

"Oh, yes," Pruitt said to the Spearmans, "the main thing is always to remove any air bubbles from the syringe. And it hurts less if the needle always goes in at an angle of ninety degrees."

"Please, Jay, don't bother Dr. Clark with your ideas about medicine." Clark looked relieved by Pamela Pruitt's admonition to her husband. The six of them settled back and contemplated the music from the steel band.

Inspector Vincent first thought that Matthew Dyke and Mrs. Doakes were leaving together. But then he saw that they had merely gotten up in order to socialize with another group. He watched the seminary professor amble over to the Pruitt's table, followed by Felicia Doakes.

"Mind if we join you?" he said, peering down his aquiline nose. Not waiting for a reply, he brought over two chairs for himself and his companion. After the conventional small talk, Professor Dyke revealed the reason for his visit.

"I have a document, Henry, which you in particular should be interested in. It nicely summarizes the economic situation on these islands."

"How did you happen upon it?" Spearman asked cautiously, for summary treatments of complex situations made him skeptical.

"Well, as you know, I have made close friends with many of the black employees at the hotel. I don't look upon them as cold statistical data for my research but rather as human beings whose social situations are of deep interest. In return for my concern, Vernon Harbley, one of our waiters, gave me a copy of the newsletter which clandestinely circulates among some of the help. Interestingly, the newsletter is put out by the very person who is entertaining us tonight. It's no coincidence that the arrival of the newsletter on St. John always occurs on a day when the Raiders perform here."

Professor Spearman was handed a slick pamphlet entitled the *Raider*. Dyke directed his attention to the article he wanted him to read. Spearman's eyes, not especially sharp even in good light, scanned the assignment with difficulty in the candlelit atmosphere.

"I see our artist tonight is somewhat of a Marxist," Professor Spearman concluded, looking up from the pamphlet. What had led Spearman to this deduction was Le-Mans's theory of social unrest in the Virgin Islands as explained in the article. Most observers had reasoned that the importation of alien blacks from the impoverished Dutch, French, British and independent West Indies was caused by a refusal of the native Virgin Islanders to accept anything but white-collar jobs. Consequently most of the tasks requiring manual labor were performed by aliens. The enormous economic boom which began in the mid-nineteen fifties increased the demand for these workers to such an extent that aliens now comprised almost fifty percent of the labor force and it was not uncommon for them to earn more than native Virgin Islanders, although they were not citizens and could not vote. The natives, who applied the perjorative term *garrots* to the aliens, expressed considerable resentment towards these people, and as a consequence black was set against black in a struggle for economic supremacy.

To LeMans, this conflict was misguided. The real struggle should be black against white. For he argued in the pamphlet that the system of bringing in outsiders as manual laborers was devised in order to keep the wages of native Virgin Islanders down and in this way cause a division within the ranks of the black population. The point was that the white businessmen, by bringing this cheap source of labor to the islands, could keep wages low and make enormous profits. And because the black workers made such low wages, they could not afford to own land on their own islands, which was being bought up by wealthy continentals.

"What makes you say he's a Marxist?"

"Surely you recognize this argument as nothing more than the old Marxian notion that capitalists require a reserve army of unemployed in order to keep wages low. In this case the role of the reserve army is played by the imported alien labor. When you combine this with Le-Mans's view of a class struggle, you have the standard elements of the Marxian motif."

"Calling the argument Marxian," Dyke objected, "doesn't make it wrong. And in fact I have always interpreted Marx as a humanitarian who cared more about the wages of workers than the profits of businessmen. How else can you account for these businessmen bringing in alien workers?"

"There is another explanation that comes to mind," Spearman replied, making one of his lecturing gestures, "and it does not require that the hundreds of businessmen on the islands engage in any conspiratorial or exploitive behavior."

"And what is that explanation?"

"Simply that the alien workers come here to improve their lot. Living on islands where their economic status and future is bleak, they voluntarily emigrate to the Virgin Islands, where wages, although low by the standards of a divinity school professor, are nevertheless high compared to their alternatives at home."

"Well, even if it is the case that the aliens come here voluntarily," Dyke narrowed his eyes and looked at Spearman, "Wouldn't you agree that it is unethical for the businessmen on the islands to take advantage of them in the manner they do? After all, they could take lower profits and pay them higher wages."

"Are you saying that profit-maximizing behavior is unethical?" Spearman asked in reply.

"Yes," he said baldly.

At this point Mrs. Felicia Doakes could not restrain herself from entering the conversation, and she turned to Matthew Dyke. "Oh, I hope that isn't so, because I just learned the other day from Dr. Spearman that I'm a profit-maximizing capitalist when I price my cookbooks."

Only nodding an acknowledgment of Mrs. Doake's interjection in the discussion, Spearman moved forward in his seat. Being short, he had difficulty making his feet touch the floor. "I cannot comment on whether maximizing one's profits is unethical or not, but I have observed that it is a very common trait of mankind. Divinity professors have even been known to exhibit this characteristic."

Professor Dyke had the sinking feeling that he was about to come out again on the losing end of a debate with his colleague. But it was too late to retreat. "If that oblique reference is to me, when have I engaged in profit-maximizing behavior?"

"As I recall, you had a sabbatical a year ago, did you not?"

"Oh, you mean when I went to Edinburgh?"

"I guess that's the time. Well, anyway, you sublet your house to a visiting professor in the economics department. He got the house by offering you a higher rent than anyone else was willing to pay. But you would agree, certainly, that there were many impecunious graduate students at Harvard who would have been happy to have rented your house at a lower price. Yet you took no less in renting your house than you could get. This is not any different in principle from the businessman who pays no more than necessary to hire his employees." Spearman paused, took a bite of the pineapple wedge that garnished his drink, then continued. "For that matter, the university's provost tells me that your colleagues in the divinity school show the same ardor in negotiating salary increases as any other professors at the campus. Perhaps I have been inattentive to all that goes on, but I have yet to hear of anybody on your faculty ever requesting a salary decrease."

Professor Dyke, unaccustomed to being without a reply, smiled wanly and retreated to his planter's punch.

Franklin Vincent was filling his pipe for the second time. The animated conversation which he had been observing seemed to have subsided, and his attention was drawn to the table occupied by Laura Burk. The primly dressed loner was in the process of signing her bill, and she then rose from her chair and started in the inspector's direction. Miss Burk appeared to be leaving, and Vincent struggled to think if there were additional questions he should ask her. Before he could decide, the sinewy young woman stopped abruptly at the table of Mr. and Mrs. Foote and began to converse with the Justice.

Vincent strained to hear the conversation which ensued, but he could catch nothing of the preliminaries. The distance from their table was only a minor part of the problem. The steel band was inopportunely playing one of their more boisterous numbers, and this in particular made his endeavors difficult. He moved diagonally to his left to position himself behind one of the supporting columns of the pavilion's cover, not daring to go any closer for fear of being noticed.

"... jog every day along those paths," Vincent thought he could hear the Justice saying. Laura Burk's reply was inaudible. She was in animated discussion on something or other that obviously was of great importance to her. Suddenly she reached into her purse and thrust what looked to Vincent to be a photograph under Curtis Foote's gaze. Inspector Vincent stood on his tiptoes trying to discern the image that had clearly captured the Justice's interest. But to no avail. Laura Burk left the Foote's table and hurried out into the night.

The detective from Cruz Bay hesitated once again while trying to make up his mind whether he should follow Laura Burk. His momentary indecision permitted him to partake of a domestic squabble that he had not anticipated. Curtis Foote was excitedly showing the photograph to his wife and said something that sounded to Vincent like "... in my log." Whatever it was, he had elicited a harsh response from his wife. As they exchanged words, their voices became loud enough to carry over the sounds of the band and for a few moments Vincent had no trouble distinguishing what was being said.

"So obvious, darling. Really, I thought you had more imagination. At least out of respect for me you might make your liaisons more clandestine."

At that moment Vernon Harbley's figure blocked the inspector's view as he brought two drinks to their table. The contretemps was interrupted until the waiter left.

"I can assure you I never saw her before in my life. And it should be evident even to you I did not invite her to our table." He tapped the back of his fingers against the photograph as he handed it to his wife. "This was no ruse; that lady was serious."

"Well, when you enter all this in your log, I trust you will record her telephone number and dimensions for posterity's sake." She took the photograph and stared at it for a moment.

Foote was visibly exasperated by his wife's attitude. "You distort everything. Can't you understand how important this could be to her? When I get back to our room I'm going to check this against the entry in my log."

"Is that an entry of what you actually saw or is it like the other entry concerning the murder?" By this time their voices had lowered to an exaggerated whisper so those at nearby tables had difficulty digesting the words of the argument. Some, like Doug and Judy Clark, appeared embarrassed by it all. Others, like Professor Spearman, looked more circumspect as they strained to hear.

Listening became easier as the Footes' voices rose above a whisper again. "You used to record only what actually happened. Lately you've been writing in what you imagine."

"Ginger, there is an enormous difference between observation and imagination."

Then a cessation of the music seemed to make the Footes aware of the level of their fulminations. Inspector Vincent, along with most of the others at the scene, watched them both fall into silence as the Raiders ended their first set. During the break, Professor Spearman amused himself by casually flipping the pages of the pamphlet which Professor Dyke had left with him. He was particularly interested to see if any businesses carried advertisements, which might explain how the publication was financed. When he reached the back page of the issue, he noticed a drawing of a face which had become familiar to him. It was crudely done but unmistakable. Under the heading TARGET was the name and face of Curtis Foote. The TARGET of this issue read as follows:

> If you are wondering why millions live in poverty and others can grow rich off their labor, the decisions of Judge Curtis Foote provide an important answer. From the day he entered politics, he voted in favor of every procapitalist and oppressive piece of legislation and voted against every bill which would bring equality and justice to the poor. Four years ago the President appointed this racist to the Supreme Court. Since then he has tried to take back the few crumbs that blacks had received from the government. His decisions show his insensibilities to our plight and his disregard for our fight for justice and black power. Now he has resigned to run for the presidency with the backing of fascist and racist elements in the United States.
>
> Brothers and sisters, Curtis Foote and his wife are our guests in the islands. They are staying on St. John in cottage #32 at Cinnamon Bay. Treat them well.

After reading the provocative profile, Spearman was disturbed. Such an attack could easily inspire a fanatic to take extreme measures against Foote or his wife. He felt that Foote should be made aware of this possibility in case he wanted to take any necessary precautions.

Returning the pamphlet to its owner, he said to Professor Dyke, "Have you read the back page of the paper you gave me?"

"Yes, I have. Hits the bull's-eye, doesn't it? Three of

my former students are in jail because of him. They are
the ones that tried to liberate a White House guard station. Almost alone that prairie fascist has been responsible for the suppression of the civil disobedience movement."

"Well, be that as it may, I am concerned that he be
made aware of this. Don't you think you should show this
to him?"

"I see no reason why that cannot be done," Dyke replied. "Perhaps I'll have the opportunity to educate him
about ethical justice." Professor Dyke retrieved the paper
from Spearman, tucked it into his jacket pocket, and
sauntered over to the Justice.

"Justice Foote, allow me to introduce myself. I am Professor Matthew Dyke of the Harvard Divinity School. I
have some information that might be of interest to you."

Curtis Foote was obviously still perturbed over the dispute he had been having with his wife, and so he wel-
comed the opportunity which this interruption afforded
to reduce the tensions at his table. He knew that Virginia's moods, which were mercurial, could be easily
shifted by the presence of a stranger. Foote offered a chair
to the professor and at the same time turned to his wife
and said, "Darling, this is Mr. Matthew Dyke, you may
recall his name, the fellow who advocates the new immorality. Professor Dyke, this is my wife, Virginia Foote."

Dyke was already seated as he acknowledged this in-
troduction. But he had mixed feelings about the remark.
He was flattered that his work was known by Foote and
pleased to meet the Justice's elegant wife. But the term
new immorality grated on him. It seemed like an unfair
distortion of the title of his book.

Foote offered to buy Dyke a drink, but before the latter could respond, the Justice explained to his wife, "This is the professor who tells us it is all right, indeed *ethical*, to kill, cheat, lie, and steal, but of course *only* if the demands of love dictate such mayhem and havoc." Then turning back to his guest, he went on: "I don't want to do an injustice to the work of such a profound theologian. Is that a fair interpretation of your position?"

At this point Mrs. Foote interjected, "Why, what a perfectly intriguing philosophy. Do you have any situations in which it would be ethically proper for a wife to murder her husband?" Her glance turned from Dyke, and she smiled at her husband in exaggerated sweetness.

By this time Dyke feigned no expressions or tones of amiability. "I did not come here to play games about ethics, an area in which your husband's whole career has demonstrated his insensitivity. I came here at the suggestion of someone who felt you ought to be aware of the contents of this pamphlet. It is authored by the person who is entertaining you tonight." Dyke left the pamphlet on the table. Then he rose, turned sharply on his heels, and stalked out of the pavilion in the direction of his room.

As Dyke was leaving, the Raiders, who had reassembled after the intermission, were beginning their last set. But it was not until the closing theme song of the band that the Justice noticed the image of himself on the back of the pamphlet. As the band played "Yellow Bird," Justice Foote read the profile and again became visibly upset. At the conclusion of the number, he angrily approached Ricky LeMans.

"I resent this libelous attack on my character," Foote

said. "If you were in my court, I would hold you in contempt."

"But in these islands, I am not in your court. You are in my brothers' and sisters' court. And it is a court with nothing but contempt for you."

9

THE NARROW WINDING STREETS of Charlotte Amalie reflected the city's past. Architecturally not much had changed since pirates dropped anchor in the harbor, slave traders engaged in their sale of human cargo, and Danish plantation owners exported the sugar cane, which they called white gold. The character of the town had been maintained in its old churches, fortifications, and government houses. Dronningens Gade was the main shopping street in Charlotte Amalie. Many of the shops along Dronningens Gade were located in old warehouses left over from the days when the town became known as "the emporium of the West Indies." For Charlotte Amalie had been a port of such size that many warehouses were required to handle the inventories that flowed through her harbor.

The Spearmans had decided to spend the day here, having taken advantage of the hotel's weekly excursion to this port city on the island of St. Thomas. Like all visitors, they were enjoying the excitement of the bustling hillside city, and one did not have to be an economist to enjoy the low prices of the wares sold in its shops.

"Why are there so many more things for sale here than in Boston?" Mrs. Spearman asked.

"There are certainly more items in total for sale in Boston than are available here. But you are really asking a different question; you are asking about the enormous variety of goods relative to the island's population. And that question is a good one."

"And what's the answer?" she inquired, as her eyes scanned an incredible variety of lotions in a corner perfumery.

"St. Thomas, like Boston, is a port city. But there's a significant distinction between the two. This is a free port—one of the few left in the world. That means that there are no import duties on anything sold here. Some of the items are unavailable back home because foreign producers cannot pay the tariff and still find a profitable market in America. That is why you see such an extensive selection of china and glassware."

As a man interested in prices, Henry Spearman was having a feast. For in few places in the world were the effects of government-imposed tariffs and duties so evident. His curiosity about the inventory displayed in a jeweler's window was such that he flattened his nose against the pane, much as a child might outside a candy store.

"Look at this, Pidge. Here is a Nivada Chronomaster selling for fifty-nine dollars—it would be one hundred ten in Boston."

But Mrs. Spearman was preoccupied, her eyes riveted on a truly dazzling timepiece—a solid jade dial encircled by diamonds with a gold bracelet. It was a Piaget. "I adore that watch. But look at the price." It was two thousand twenty-five dollars. "Could that be even more in Boston?" she asked.

Professor Spearman estimated. "That watch would

sell for at least three thousand five hundred dollars in Boston or New York."

As they maneuvered down the busy main street, Professor Spearman was not surprised to see similar price differentials on cameras, luggage, jewelry, liquor, and tobacco. Stopping inside the shop of a tobacconist, Spearman decided to purchase a gift for a favored colleague with whom he had coauthored his renowned treatise on the theory of prices.

"I would like to buy two boxes of the Carl Upmann cigars, the ones in the Honduran mahogany cases." Spearman had noticed in the window that they sold for fifty-five percent less than his colleague paid at the tobacconist near the Harvard Yard.

"Have you seen our selection from the Canary Islands?" the clerk suggested helpfully.

"I don't smoke. I'm purchasing the Upmanns for a friend, and that is his brand."

"Your friend must be a connoisseur," the clerk remarked as he bagged the items.

"Let us say he has expensive tastes," Spearman replied dryly.

Having made the purchase, the Spearmans took their lunch on the veranda of the picturesque Grand Hotel, not only the island's oldest hotel, but also the longest continuously operating hotel under the U.S. flag. From their table they could see not only the harbor but also the hilly countryside dotted with pastel houses. Before lunch they enjoyed the hotel's famous banana daiquiri.

Mrs. Spearman seemed pensive. She was a woman who usually took little interest in economics, but an idea had crossed her mind. "Henry, why doesn't someone buy up the merchandise here, since it is so inexpensive, and resell it in Boston at a big profit?"

"Another subtle question about economics!" He stirred some sugar into his coffee. "If someone did what you suggested, that would be called arbitrage. Eventually the process of buying in Charlotte Amalie and selling in Boston would raise prices here but lower them there until any price difference between the two cities would reflect only the transportation cost. As residents of the Boston area, this would be to our great advantage."

"Why don't we do it then?" she asked.

"Because we would go to jail if we tried," quipped Spearman. "Although there are no duties or restrictions on goods imported into St. Thomas, the government limits the amount of articles we can take home with us. If we were to return with more than four hundred dollars worth of merchandise, we would have to pay a customs duty. This duty makes artibrage unprofitable." Finishing his coffee Spearman tried to catch the waiter's eye.

"Why would our government do that?" Pidge asked, as a waiter approached with their bill.

"I am afraid that governments do not always operate in the interests of all their citizens. In order to promote the interests of one group, in this case businessmen, governments often impose severe costs upon another group, in this case consumers."

Leaving the hotel, they began walking in the direction of the old post office, where there was a taxi stand. Pidge wanted to visit the orchidarium west of town. Approaching them on the street was a group of six black youths. They had formed a menacing row astride the narrow passageway, as if to defiantly challenge anyone to pass

by them. It was with great difficulty and considerable trep-
idation that the Spearmans were able to continue up the
street.

"Hey man, you hadn't better be back on this street
after dark," one of the more hostile looking of the young
men taunted.

Mrs. Spearman was rather visibly shaken. After the
youths were out of earshot she asked, "Why would they
talk that way to us?"

"That is symptomatic of the racial tension in the islands and explains why fewer tourists are visiting here
these days," he replied as he opened the door of a waiting
cab. They were taken to the orchidarium, which Spearman visited with his wife until it was time to return to the
hotel's launch for the trip back to St. John.

Captain Arvel Blaylock was waiting on the dock at
the Red Hook landing for the hotel's guests whom he had
brought over that morning for the day's excursion to
Charlotte Amalie. Blaylock, whose appearance was an
amalgam of his environment, was a favorite with the
guests. A dark, leathery face bespoke many days at sea; his
protruding potbelly suggested many nights in waterfront
saloons. As a young man he had skippered a merchant
marine ship that paid calls on many Caribbean ports. But
at his present age he had settled most comfortably into
the routine of skippering the hotel's Grand Banks trawler
between St. John and St. Thomas.

At five p.m. Blaylock pulled the whistle cord above
the skipper's wheel to announce that it was time to board
the boat. He knew there would be three arriving guests in
addition to the seven who had been on the shopping tour.
When they were all accounted for, he signalled for his

crew to cast off. Then he guided the boat slowly out of the small harbor at the east end of the island. Once in open water he turned the wheel over to one of the two crew members and went below to welcome the newcomers and chat with the returning shoppers. Captain Blaylock always had fun with those who came back laden with overflowing shopping bags and cartons of liquor. He kidded them gently about spending all their money and going home broke. One couple, sitting in the stern of the boat, for instance, had so many packages that the captain decided to warn them that they were causing the boat to list dangerously. He had used this line before and knew that the guests appreciated this mild-mannered kidding. Some even tittered with embarrassment.

To starboard were a man and wife he had noticed this morning and who now stymied the amiable captain. Their laps were not encumbered with many packages, and they had no shopping bags at their feet.

"Looks like you earned lots of money today!" he chortled to the couple.

"Why do you say that?" the husband asked

"A penny saved is a penny earned and it looks like you saved a lot of pennies today. You keep this up, and the merchants are going to have supplies they can't sell."

"No, no," replied Professor Spearman, "Say's Law teaches us that a penny saved is a penny spent. So you needn't worry about the merchandise. Supply creates its own demand."

Captain Blaylock, not being a Keynesian, was unaware of an appropriate response to the professor's singularly classical proposition, but he pretended to agree with it by nodding his head and smiling knowingly. Then he said, to no one in particular, "Will you folks excuse me? I think I should tell the steward it's time to serve the tea." The captain headed towards the galley.

A few moments later one of the two crew members appeared, this time in the role of a steward. The handsome young black had donned a white jacket and was balancing a circular tray of iced tea. The ice clicked in the glasses as he made his way among the passengers.

The Spearmans declined to purchase tea on this particular trip to the hotel. Both of them were more tired than thirsty. In fact, with the drone of the engines and the fresh sea air, Professor Spearman was beginning to doze off. But his nap was aborted by a commotion at the other end of the launch. One of the new arrivals, it appeared, was loudly protesting the price of the iced tea.

"I was not told by my travel agent that there would be an extra charge for refreshments."

The ebony-faced youth first looked surprised. The hotel's clientele normally did not present him with this type of protest. Then he retorted, "I don't set the hotel's policy, sir. Don't complain to me; complain to the owner." But the surly fellow was not appeased.

Spearman noted a graying man with a prognathous jaw whose face was flushed with anger, its redness contrasting against the white of a linen jacket. That there was an extra charge for the tea had angered him and his pique was now aggravated by what he considered the waiter's flippant reply.

"Where I come from you wouldn't talk like that." For only a second, a look of intense animosity flashed across the waiter's face, but he turned away and walked into the forward cabin. The imperious fellow turned to a young couple sitting adjacent to him and continued his mutterings. "A dollar for a glass of tea; in Atlanta you can get bourbon for that price." The young couple, probably honeymooners, nodded in astonished agreement. They appeared embarrassed to have made the purchase themselves.

Captain Blaylock, who earlier had taken over the helm of the boat, had missed the unpleasantness below. He generally piloted the boat himself after the choppy waters of the sound were crossed in order to personally handle the docking of the craft. As the hotel's dock was approached, he expertly reversed the engines and slid the vessel alongside until the boat's fenders were gently compressed against the dock's siding. When the boat was tied secure and the passenger plank in place, the young lady from the hotel came aboard to call out the names of the newcomers and check off the arriving guests against her rolls.

"Mr. and Mrs. Johnston?" she intoned cheerily.

"Right here," the presumed honeymooners responded.

"Nice to have you with us; the registration desk is straight ahead." The girl pointed down the dock toward the hotel entrance.

"And how about Mr. Fitzhugh, Mr. Bethuel Fitzhugh?" she chirped.

The gruff fellow who had been in the argument sat for a moment, then looked up and said, "Oh, you must mean me. I'm Fitzhugh."

"Welcome to Cinnamon Bay, Mr. Fitzhugh. We hope your visit with us is pleasant in every way."

10

SPEARMAN SHOWED UP EARLY at the hotel dock to rent some fins. He had decided to explore around some of the points bordering Turtle Bay and had been advised to wear fins to protect against swift currents. His swimwear that day was typical of what continentals took to be stylish attire for the Caribbean. But actually his garb was more fitting for Hawaii. On his five-foot-three physique his swimsuit gave the appearance of baggy bermudas.

The equipment steward was occupied in preparing aqualungs for the hotel's more adventuresome guests, who used them to explore the outlying coral reefs. Hearing Spearman enter the shed, the tall, boney attendant look up inquiringly. "I want to do some snorkeling and was told at the desk that I could acquire a pair of fins here."

"What size shoe do you wear?" the equipment steward asked.

Spearman scrutinized the selection of fins in the shed before replying. "Size six, but I would like to try some on to get a proper fit. Are they all the same price?"

The attendant finished putting a regulator on a pair of tanks as he replied: "The fins are free, but there's a thirty-dollar deposit. If you want a mask and snorkel, that's another twenty dollars down. You pay the deposit in cash now and you get it back when you return them."

Spearman seemed disappointed. "Cash? Hasn't the hotel changed its policy on this? In the past I recall being allowed to charge everything to my room."

"Yes, but the hotel found that they couldn't handle the bookkeeping on swim equipment at the main office because people always were returning them just before they checked out and paid their bill." Spearman located a pair of Memrod floating fins in the size six bin which seemed to match his own mask and snorkel. He gave the attendant three tens from his wallet.

"Would you sign here?" The steward held out a clipboard. Spearman picked up a pencil and wrote out his name. He pocketed his receipt and gathered the equipment. As he was leaving, he was jostled aside by a chap brusquely entering the shed. In a gruff Southern accent, the rude jostler demanded attention. "How much does it cost to rent a pair of fins for the day?"

Spearman noticed it was the same greying man who was responsible for the contretemps on the boat the day before. Anticipating another argument over prices, he lingered outside the door.

"The deposit is thirty dollars, but there's no rental charge. If you need a mask and snorkel, that's an extra twenty-dollar deposit."

"I don't want a mask and snorkel, and thirty dollars as a deposit is highway robbery. These fins retail in the states for less than that. Let me buy them outright."

"Can't do that. The hotel only allows me to loan equipment here. But you'll get your money back when you return the fins."

Cursing to himself, the surly Southerner grudgingly selected a pair of fins and threw thirty dollars on the counter. Then an obviously irritated Bethuel Fitzhugh signed his name to the receipt and stormed out of the equipment shed, jostling Spearman again on his way out.

Returning to his room, Spearman announced to his wife that he was going snorkeling around Turtle Bay. Pidge who preferred to investigate the gardens, reminded him, "Be careful where you swim. Remember that you're not a strong swimmer, and you know what they say about the currents."

"Don't worry; I'll be cautious," he replied as he left their cottage and made his way purposely for the water.

Just as he reached the wet, closely packed sand, he noticed that the beach that morning was occupied by only one other person. About twenty feet from where he was standing at the water's edge, and on Spearman's left, Mr. Bethuel Fitzhugh could be seen sunbathing on a chaise longue. The economist nodded politely in that direction and then considered the problem before him: putting on his equipment.

Spearman had observed that when it came to donning swim fins people could be divided into two camps. One group, which he had dubbed the amphibians, squatted down on the beach and struggled to pull the dry rubber over each instep. Once the fins were in place members of this camp had to be able to walk as if their feet had taken on the proportions of an enormous bird. This required either an exaggerated lifting of the feet if moving forward or, as some soon learned walking backwards with short sliding steps into the water. Spearman considered the chief disadvantage of this approach to be the irritation caused by the sand particles which inevitably lodged themselves between the stretched rubber and one's feet.

The second camp, the aquatics, avoided these problems by accomplishing the entire operation within the water. But in order to be a candidate here one had to engage in a calisthenic not open to the less agile. The prerequisite was the ability either to balance on one leg in wavy water while inserting a submerged but buoyant fin onto the foot or, alternatively, holding one's breath, going into a tuck, and then deftly engaging the fin's aperture with the point of the foot. Spearman admired the aquatics but was congenitally an amphibian. He plopped down to put on his fins before entering the water.

Swimming more rapidly than usual, he made his way toward the reef that separated his bay from Scott Beach. When he reached the point, he paddled over to observe some brain coral, whose patterns were similar to the convolutions of the human cerebrum. After about an hour's time he tired and began to make his way back to the shore. As he approached shallow water, he experienced a slight degree of apprehension as a sideways glance revealed a large gray stingray hovering over the sandy bottom. Spearman half-swam, half-floated over the ray and watched its seemingly unsystematic scavenging along the ocean floor. As he did so he heard the whining drone of a passing power boat. He poked his head up and saw in the distance the blue hull of the *Bomba Challenger* on its way to Tortola. Spearman turned onto his back and waited for the power boat's wake to carry him onto the shore.

As he dried himself he could not help but notice that he was now alone on the beach; only a towel and an open bottle of tanning lotion remained on the chaise longue earlier occupied by Bethuel Fitzhugh.

The old estate house, with its veranda now serving as a cocktail pavilion, was situated in a horticulturist's heaven. Poincianas, bougainvilleas, and fiery hibiscus provided an environment not unlike paradise, which the hotel guests could appreciate while chatting and drinking. But tonight they were not doing so with their usual amiability. There was one topic from which the conversation did not long stray, namely the drowning of one of the hotel's guests. Of this tragedy Professor Spearman was not yet aware.

As he and his wife climbed the old stone steps to the terrace, he was somewhat puzzled by the subdued tones of the gathering. They selected a table that allowed them a spectacular vista of the evening's sunset. It was their favorite table.

"Isn't it just terrible about the drowning? My word, Harold, had I known there were strong currents out there I never would have gone swimming this afternoon." The voice was that of a lady seated at a cocktail table immediately adjacent to the Spearmans.

Professor Spearman looked over and saw an older woman wearing a silk pantsuit of pastel shades. She was speaking to her husband, an impeccably dressed gentleman in a blue blazer who appeared to be several years her junior. Crushing his cigarette into the ashtray, he said, "Cynthia, there is a sign on our beach which warns of the currents." He paused, then added, "But like all caution signs, one thinks they apply only to others."

"Well what good is a sign warning of strong currents? You wouldn't know you were in one until it was too late, would you?"

"Maybe not," he replied. "But I wouldn't think they would be much of a problem if one were a good swimmer, particularly if one were wearing fins."

"But they say he *was* wearing fins. The equipment

steward claimed he had rented him a pair just the day he drowned. The sad thing is no one knew he was even missing until the cleaning woman reported that his bed remained unslept in last night."

"You mean he was here all alone?"

"It appears so. All I heard is that he came in two days ago from Georgia."

Overhearing all this, Professor Spearman looked over to his wife and then turned to the person addressed as Harold and said, "Pardon my intrusion, but I couldn't help overhearing some of your remarks. Is it possible that the drowned man was lost off Turtle Bay?"

"Yes," Harold replied, turning his angular face in the Spearman's direction. "They found some of his possessions on the beach there. How did you know?"

"Because I saw him there that very morning." Spearman turned back to his table, and his wife noticed a look of puzzlement cross his face. He thought for some time and then turned and inquired. "Have they found the body?"

"No," Cynthia shuddered; "the police say that bodies lost in these waters may not turn up for several days, if at all. They can drift for a long time or get caught in coral or even eaten by sharks."

One person apparently neither preoccupied nor moved by the drowning was Professor Dyke. Spotting the Spearmans, he ambled over to them and as he pulled up a chair, asked if he could join them. Not awaiting a reply, he then said, "I see you do not yet have drinks. Will you be my guest for some?"

"We will each have a pineapple daiquiri," Spearman replied.

It should be noted that the short economist did not

consider himself to be the recipient of unilateral largesse. A fundamental principle of economics is that there is no such thing as a free lunch. Spearman knew that a major cost of these drinks would be his seemingly respectful attention to whatever Dyke planned to make the subject of that evening's symposium. This cost was somewhat offset by Spearman's being able to note that Dyke's propensity to appear generous had an inverse relationship to the lateness of the hour. Spearman mused that this was just one more confirmation of the law of demand. During the five-to-six hospitality hour, Dyke displayed a willingness to buy more drinks both for himself and others. As the sun set and the shadows lengthened, he jettisoned the role of host and reduced his own liquid intake. But he still exacted the attention of his audience.

Of course, Dyke would consider the word "exacted" inappropriate. After all, he was paid well to lecture before various denominational groups, seminaries, and universities ever since the publication of his celebrated book on ethics. So he had come to believe that everyone would like to hear his views on this, his favorite subject. It would be unkind, he thought, to deny the Spearmans a chance to discuss the topic with him.

As the waiter left with the drink order, Dyke took the opportunity afforded by a lull in the conversation to inquire as to whether the famed economist had read his book on contextual ethics.

"I'm afraid the central theme escapes me at the moment," Spearman replied. He had in fact not read the book, but he hesitated to ask Dyke for its main argument. Spearman had often observed the curious inability of academics to be able to describe orally in a succinct fashion the contents of their own books and articles. But Dyke did not wait for an invitation.

"In my book, I demonstrate how adherence to absolute principles can in certain contexts lead to unethical results. I believe that some of the great injustices have occurred because the churches of the Western world have, on the grounds of either Scripture or natural theology, mistakenly elevated certain moral maxims into ethical absolutes. There are no absolute rules. Man cannot hold to absolute rules and still retain his modernity. In fact, I would think the rationality of my ethic, which has gained a wide following in theology, would hold particular appeal to economists, given their affinity for rationality."

"Why do you say your ethic is rational?" Spearman asked.

"Because it gives modern man a rule applicable to the different situations in which he finds himself. Traditional Judeo-Christian ethics gave him an absolute. For example: thou shalt not steal. This strikes modern man as irrational since he knows at times stealing could be an ethical act. Existential antinomianism ethics gives him another absolute: no standard. It doesn't matter what you do, simply affirm yourself in the action. This also strikes modern man as irrational since he knows it would lead to moral anarchy and injustice. Contextual ethics shows that whether or not one should steal ultimately depends upon the situation one is in.

Professor Spearman expressed his puzzlement. "Where is the decision rule? How am I, or you, or a judge, or a cleaning woman for that matter, to know what is ethical in any particular situation?" Spearman thought he knew what the response would be but he waited to hear it articulated.

The attendant, who had unobtrusively approached their table, inquired, "I believe the lady has the pineapple daiquiri?"

"That's right, and the other daiquiri goes there, and I'm having my usual, the planter's punch," Dyke answered.

Dyke paused until the drinks had been served before continuing. "What determines the response is the *end*. It is the end that justifies the particular situational means. I argue that the only legitimate end is love, or what we theologians call 'agape.' This can justify *any* means, in fact it sanctifies and redeems the means. One simply asks the question in each situation: what does love demand of me here?"

Spearman's brow knitted. "And how do I know what is loving?" he inquired.

"One is loving when one does something for the good of others. In the area of social justice, it is not totally unlike the utilitarian ethics of Bentham and Mill, with whom you are no doubt familiar. But they were confused because they saw no divine aspect to the ethic. The divine aspect is love, one does whatever brings goodness to others."

This is the part that bothered Spearman. As an economist, he recognized the scientific difficulties in knowing the combination of goods and services that most productively contributed to the happiness of another. To maximize one's own utility was one thing; to maximize that of another was considered conceptually impossible.

But before he could marshall his thoughts to explain

them to Dyke, the latter went on. "A great virtue of what I call the new morality is its resolving both personal and social ethical dilemmas. For example, the Bible is sometimes interpreted as saying 'One shall not kill.' But under a contextual standard, President Truman's decision to bomb Hiroshima was an ethical one. The decision was not 'just' because it contributed to the nation's defense and security; the decision was not 'just' because Japan was the aggressor nation in the Pacific war. Love dictated the bombing in order to stop the war. The decision was loving, for by shortening the war, more lives were saved than lost in the bombing.

"Let us say the Japanese had first developed nuclear weapons. Since it would also likely have stopped the war, would it have been just as ethical if the Japanese had dropped atomic bombs on New York and Boston?"

Professor Dyke thought for awhile and then admitted, though Spearman detected with no enthusiasm, that this too would have been an ethical act.

"Why will people act out of this motive of love?" Spearman asked.

"That is why I write popular books," Professor Dyke replied with missionary zeal. "Education and persuasion will someday induce loving behavior."

Spearman usually assumed individuals operated in their self-interest, not out of love. And while he attached no moral connotation to the self-interest assumption, he was troubled by Dyke's assertion that people could be motivated solely by love. For many years an agnostic, he was reminded of a Bible verse from Hebrew school: "The heart is deceitful above all things, and desperately wicked." The verse struck a responsive chord, and he thought to himself that someday he would have to re-think certain theological issues.

But in the meantime, the theologian droned on about situations where coveting, lying, adultery, and stealing could be justified. Like a good actor he saved his best material for the last: his familiar examples of when even murder could be justified. As Professor Dyke liked to put it, "The sixth commandment ought really to be: Thou shalt not murder, except in extenuating curcumstances where love allows, indeed requires, the act."

"Are you saying that in certain circumstances premeditated murder is ethically justifiable?"

"Under certain circumstances, yes."

11

LAURA BURK twisted the point of the broad-bladed implement into the crevice of a rock. The pressure she exerted
on the blade began to bend the tool's shank. It was early
afternoon and very hot on the Hawksnest Point trail. Her
khaki shirt was soaked with moisture, and the perspira-
tion from her brow blurred her vision momentarily. Retrieving a towel from her bag she wiped her face. Even the
grounds crew at the hotel did not work during this part
of the day, but Miss Burk, who appeared to have the
strength of a man, was determined.

Rummaging around in the bag, she extracted a long,
thin-bladed knife and began to probe deftly along the
same surface of the rock. She then examined her efforts
and, taking a small brush of the sort a painter might use,
whisked away the scrapings. Once again she stared at the
surface and a smile of satisfaction crossed her lips. She
picked up the small camera lying on the rubberoid sheet
by her knees and prepared to photograph the results of her
efforts.

But before she could snap the picture, she suddenly
turned her head in the direction of the trail. Was it her
imagination, or did she hear the sound of someone ap-

proaching? The hollow echoes from the blowpipe made it difficult to be sure. Taking no chances she picked up the paraphernalia she had brought with her and hid herself behind a large boulder just off the trail in the direction of the woods beyond. Miss Burk waited there quietly until reassured that what she heard was probably nothing more than a branch which had fallen from a distant tree. She emerged from her hiding place and resumed her singular activities.

A magnifying glass was used to make an even more careful study of the crevice and was then put back in its case. She stepped away from the rock and pulled a compass from the pocket of her dungarees. After taking a reading the young woman next moved toward the rock and stretched a metal tape measure across the stoney foot trail. With the tape extended, she then used the blunt end of a short-handled axe to drive two stakes into the ground, one at the base of the rock, the other on the side of the trail adjacent to the blowpipe.

But at this point she was interrupted again, this time by a sound coming unmistakably from the rocks jutting up from the water's edge. She heard noises of someone, a swimmer she thought, emerging from the water below and making his way up the rocks to the Hawksnest trail. To say that she was surprised would be an understatement. Laura Burk had been at this particular place on the path before and had never expected her labors to be broken off by anyone approaching from such a difficult if not treacherous angle. She knew that the currents around the point were unpredictable and that only a strong swimmer could safely venture this far from the island's beaches.

Hastily retrieving her gear, she made her way north

on the trail back to the hotel. As she trudged along in the sultry air she thought to herself, I must return later to finish the job.

The Spearmans waited under the shade of a yellow flamboyant tree. Professor Spearman had suggested to his wife that they visit the picturesque hamlet of Cruz Bay because, as he informed her almost sheepishly, he wanted to observe firsthand the market behavior in and around the public dock. She agreed to accompany her husband because she was attracted by the chance to visit a museum in the town whose exhibits were said to provide a good perspective on St. John's history.

One could walk to Cruz Bay along a trail leading out from the southwest side of the hotel's grounds. And many of the guests made a point of taking this hike at least once during their stay. Henry Spearman liked hiking and might have chosen that mode of transportation today, everything else being equal. But as is so often the case in human decision-making, not everything was equal.

For one thing there was the matter of time. As much as Pidge regretted it, her husband no longer seemed to be unwinding at a vacation retreat. She was only too keenly aware that the murder of General Decker had somehow come to preoccupy much of her husband's attention in the same manner that an economic puzzle might have been challenging him. Today he seemed almost as anxious to get to Cruz Bay as he was to get to his workshop in Neoclassical Economics during the school year. Therefore a leisurely trek over the steep hill that separated the hotel from the town would consume too much valuable time.

In addition, there was the matter of his wife's comfort. The trail involved rather steep climbs, and there was always some probability of tripping and falling on the stones or roots that studded the path. Spearman was not surprised to learn that there were local entrepreneurs who provided a service which was both faster and more comfortable. He had learned that a round trip to Cruz Bay in a taxi would cost four dollars for both of them. In terms of real costs, this was the more sensible alternative.

While waiting for their cab they entertained themselves by watching the antics of a stealthy mongoose scurrying among the nearby bushes. In appearance the animal was a cross between a squirrel and a weasel, but its contribution to life on the island went beyond playing the clown for the amusement of tourists. The rodent was brought to St. John in the seventeen hundreds to rid the island of rats, but a lack of synchronization in sleeping habits prevented the desired result. The diurnal mongoose and the nocturnal rat never met. But the creature more than proved his usefulness by ridding the island of snakes.

"Are you the people what want to go to Cruz Bay?" the elderly black cabbie called out as he stopped his maroon microbus in the parking lot below the sugar mill ruins. Startled, the mongoose darted away.

"That's correct," Pidge replied as they walked into the sunlight toward the vehicle.

"I understand the fare is two dollars each way," her husband said. The driver simply nodded and grunted acceptance of those terms. They clambered aboard and tried to slide the door shut, but without success.

"You have to pull on it while you shut it," the driver

explained. But Henry Spearman did not seem to have the knack, and the chauffeur got out to close the door himself.

The cab pulled out of the parking lot and proceeded through the back part of the hotel's grounds, making its way past the quarters reserved for the hotel's employees. The Spearmans both felt like intruders as they watched the help in this surrounding. But Pidge also felt some guilt. The contrast between her accommodations at the hotel and that of the help was apparent. Her spouse, on the other hand, was aware that the housing for the help at Cinnamon Bay was far better than that of the typical native islander. For Spearman, unlike Pidge, was a trained economist. He was aware that most people everywhere are hewers of wood and drawers of water. The point was, however, that the hewing of wood and the drawing of water by these St. John inhabitants were far more productive than would otherwise be the case (and their incomes consequently greater) because of the activities of the entrepreneur who undertook the path-breaking venture of creating a resort hotel on this once neglected island. Spearman believed that the history of every nation would show that a tiny percentage of the community sets the pace and promotes the economic activity of hosts of others.

The road between the hotel and Cruz Bay was a winding thoroughfare with some rather steep climbs and descents. At one place it afforded a spectacular vista of the Cruz Bay environs just before the road made its final drop into the town.

"My wife wants to visit the museum. Would you please let us off there?" Spearman asked the driver. The museum was on the lower level of the Administration House, a large, white, blocklike residence that had served as the Governor's mansion when the island was owned by Denmark. The building was set on a point which bisected the Cruz Bay harbor and now housed, in addition to island artifacts and relics, a number of government offices.

"It's just a short distance to the public dock. I'll walk from here and when you finish touring the exhibits, join me and we'll see if there's a reasonable place for lunch."

"I imagine my stay here won't be more than an hour. Will that give you enough time?" Pidge asked.

"Yes, I think in an hour I should be satisfied."

After saying good-bye, Professor Spearman sauntered over in the direction of the pier where the ferry boats between the neighboring islands made their morning and evening stops. The dock was a long concrete slab, but its starkkness had been relieved by the string of green and white plastic pennants hung from the lampposts which lined the north side of the pier.

From a distance the dock gave Spearman an impression of disorder and confusion. The noise of the calypso-accented conversation reached his ears as passengers disembarked from a ferry boat which had just arrived. Some had to fend for themselves with their cartons; others were being met by expectant friends or relatives. The composition of the crowd was not at all segregated by either age or race. Whites and blacks, kids, adults, and teenagers seemed equally involved in the proceedings. An almost carnival-like atmosphere pervaded the scene whenever a boat arrived.

What prompted the commotion at hand, Spearman learned as he made his way down the concrete, was the arrival of the *Caribe Sun Rise*, a fifty-foot steel launch which made morning and evening trips to Cruz Bay from Charlotte Amalie. Spearman was pleased to note in addition to passengers the variety of goods which had arrived on the vessel. The crew had just unloaded a television console, a chrome dining room set, an LP stove, a set of barbells, a used bookcase, suitcases of many sizes, and cartons of merchandise for the area's shops. Even a car radiator was set on the dock. And yet for each diverse item that arrived, there seemed to be an individual who was its designated recipient. Superficially what had appeared at a distance to be confusion, up close was the manifestation of amazing order.

The thought struck Spearman that the proverbial visitor from Mars, if told that our world was divided into two kinds of economies, unplanned and centrally planned, would doubtless have thought the Cruz Bay dock represented remarkable planning. Every item seemed to be matched with someone who wanted it. And yet the neat meshing of wants with goods was brought about entirely through the operation of what Adam Smith had dubbed that "simple and obvious system of natural liberty." It was one of the paradoxes of economic theory and, Spearman believed, one of its greatest discoveries, that the most orderly economies were the least planned.

The market processes on the dock reminded Spearman of a quotation he regularly shared with his classes at Harvard. In the 1850s a French economist named Frederic Bastiat told how upon a visit to Paris he realized that the entire city would soon fall victim to starvation and pillage if necessary supplies were not to reach it the next day. Yet everyone slept peacefully, their slumbers undisturbed by that frightful prospect, even though there was no single authority responsible for the delivery of these necessities. Spearman saw in Cruz Bay a microcosm of what Bastiat observed in Paris.

The economist stood alongside the blue-trimmed ferry and watched as the last person stepped off the ship. There was no doubt that he was the captain. He was the only person on the dock wearing a white visored cap, and that, along with his white shirt and khakis, reminded Spearman of the hotel's Captain Blaylock. His Hush Puppies were the only discordant note in an otherwise standard ensemble.

But to Felicia Doakes, who had just rounded the ticket booth where boat passes were purchased, there was a different, discordant note. To her, Professor Spearman seemed out of place among the dock's congregation, and she watched from the front of the dock as the professor looked up in animated conversation with the captain of the *Caribe Sun Rise*. She observed the two of them for some time until her attention was distracted by a three-second hoot on a diesel horn announcing the arrival of another vessel. This one was a converted LST, a non-passenger barge, which was capable of transporting larger items such as machinery and raw materials to St. John.

Mrs. Doakes watched with curiosity as the professor went aboard and seemed to engage in conversation with the captain of this vessel as well. When Professor Spearman disembarked from the LST, he was greeted by his female observer, who had walked up the dock.

"Professor Spearman, if I had known you were coming to Cruz Bay we could have shared a cab!"

"Oh, hello, Mrs. Doakes." Professor Spearman maneuvered himself between some chicken cages that had just arrived. "Did you know that Pidge is with me, too? She would have enjoyed your company. Right now she's visiting the museum, but I expect her along shortly."

"And why are you here, Professor?"

"At this point I'm beginning to wonder that myself! And you?"

"Oh, I come to Cruz Bay often. So many native women congregate here to shop, and I take advantage of this to quiz them about their cooking methods and to authenticate the names of certain recipes. Sometimes it takes hours just to get one recipe."

Before their conversation could proceed further, Mrs. Spearman joined her husband and General Decker's widowed cousin on the dock. The three of them exchanged pleasantries about their morning activities until the professor's attention was diverted by a hubbub on the far side of the pier.

"Unless I'm wrong, some fishermen are bringing in their morning catch."

"Oh," Mrs. Spearman exclaimed, "I'd like to see that. I got here just in time." Mrs. Doakes joined them as the couple made their way to the other side of the wharf.

Two rather old wooden rowboats, powered by outboard motors, had been moored to the dock, and the native fishermen, in calypso accents, began to bargain with the people dockside for the sale of their catch. The fish lay in the bottom of the boats, some of them still gasping. Indeed, the final measure taken before the consummation of most sales was the seller striking the fish with a stubby club before passing it up to the purchaser.

"Those will be delicious if prepared this evening."

Mrs. Doakes was in her element and spoke with all the confidence of an expert. "Especially if they are pan fried. With broiling or baking, a day's wait doesn't impair the flavor all that much. But if you are going to pan fry, no, you shouldn't delay. It's a rare opportunity to find fish this fresh. The ones with the bright yellow spots are called hinds, and you probably won't find them in your area. A good substitute though, would be grouper, which has much the same taste." Over the noise, Mrs. Doakes explained that in her cookbooks she frequently had to suggest substitutes for exotic delicacies which would not always be available outside the regions where the dishes originated. "But as long as the spices of the area are available," Mrs. Doakes maintained, "the same flavors and aromas can be duplicated, even in kitchens in Indianapolis."

Professor Spearman watched as the fishermen hawked their wares, haggled over price, struck bargains, and then deftly wired the fish together for delivery to the customer. He was reminded for the second time that morning of something Adam Smith had written—about man's natural propensity to truck, barter and exchange. His students at the university could only infrequently observe buyers and sellers in the same market location. For in their experience the forces of demand and supply more often worked themselves out through written or electronic communication. But here, as at a country auction in New England, Spearman thought, one could witness the forces of demand and supply actually moving to equilibrium. Whether for the hinds, the snapper, or even for the crabs, there would be a market clearing price.

"Isn't that one of the hotel's waiters?"

Felicia Doakes turned in response to Mrs. Spearman's question. Only a few feet away stood a black man of familiar countenance. He wore dark trousers and a white shirt and was trying to get the attention of one of the fishermen.

"Yes, I recognize him. That's Vernon Harbley, the fellow who always waited on my cousin. He usually seemed rather sullen to me, like he had a chip on his shoulder, but the General didn't seem to mind him. 'As long as he's efficient and gets the job done, that's what matters,' is what my cousin said." Her voice trailed off as she murmured, more to herself than anyone else, "Humph, my poor cousin, bless his soul, I bet wherever he is now he wishes he had listened to me about number thirteen."

"Do you suppose he comes here to buy fish for the hotel?" Mrs. Spearman inquired.

"Oh, heavens no," Mrs. Doakes retorted, her attention returning to her companions. "I've had many arguments with the hotel's management about that. The help come down here and buy fresh fish for their own meals at home. All of the fish the guests are served have been frozen! Now isn't that a sorry state of affairs?"

"Why, you would think that with fresh fish all around us, the hotel would catch them to serve to the guests," Mrs. Spearman agreed. "Are you sure the fish we eat are all bought frozen?"

"Mr. Wyatt told me that was the case. But of course he said fish tasted better that way . . . frozen, I mean. Now that's nonsense. Of course, he wanted to make me think that the guests are better off with that silly practice."

The shortest member of the trio piped up, "But the point is, they are."

"How can we be better off with frozen fish? Fresh tastes better!"

Spearman decided to qualify his statement. "But you might be better off with frozen fish if the alternative would sometimes be no fish at all." Spearman then endeavored didactically to explain the inventory problem. He pointed out that buying fish frozen guarantees a stock on hand adequate to meet the demands of all the hotel's guests, and enables the chef to plan his menu in advance. To rely on fresh fish, Spearman reasoned, would mean that the day's fish entree would be unpredictably dependent upon the day's catch. Moreover, not all of the guests could be guaranteed fish for dinner. "So you see such matters involve trade-offs. It may well be to our benefit to have the certainty of slightly less tasty fish to the uncertainty of having the more delicious but unpredictably obtainable fresh fish."

"Mr. Wyatt told me there may not be many fish around here in a few years. He said the natives are catching so many that there are not going to be enough left to reproduce themselves," Mrs. Spearman interjected.

The thought of an ocean without fish was more than Mrs. Doakes could bear. She shook her finger at Professor Spearman and admonished him, "Isn't this fish situation simply the end result of your profit maximizing? Now I see why Professor Dyke dislikes capitalism."

"Profit maximizing, yes; capitalism, no," Spearman softly replied. "Let me explain. In order for capitalism to serve the public's interest, there must be private property. Each seller and each buyer then has a keen personal incentive to maximize the value of that which he uses or sells. Dyke is correct in believing that it is profit maximizing behavior that leads fishermen to overfish the water. But this poses a problem only because the water does not belong to anyone in particular. Far from capitalism leading greedy profit seekers to overfish, it is the lack of the chief feature of capitalism, namely private property, which is the root cause of your concern."

Mrs. Doakes objected that she thought profit maximizing and capitalism were one and the same.

"Not at all! The Cuban trawlers, surely not capitalistic ships, are every bit as anxious to get the fish from the ocean as the fishermen we see at this dock. If capitalism existed no place in the world, you would face the same problem. On the other hand, if capitalism existed everywhere in the world, that is literally even including the oceans, the problem would not exist at all."

The so-called economics of the common pool was one of Spearman's research interests, and as he warmed to his subject he drew on a favorite classroom example. "You'll notice that Mr. Wyatt is apparently not concerned about the world running out of beef. Why fish and not beef? Because ownership of beef is clearly defined; there is a strong incentive to maintain a continuing profitable supply. But no individual fisherman has such an incentive. A fish not caught and sold by one fisherman might be caught and sold by another."

"That's very interesting, Dr. Spearman. You must tell all this to Professor Dyke. He might even come around to your point of view."

"I'm sure he shares my point of view that the oceans should not be overfished; what he lacks, I suspect, are the theoretical tools to analyze the problem."

The three hotel guests remained on the Cruz Bay

wharf for another twenty minutes or so, chatting and watching. During this time the busyness on the pier subsided as the morning ferries left for other islands and the fishermen sold what remained of their first catch of the day.

"Do you think we can find a good place to eat in Cruz Bay?" Pidge Spearman asked Mrs. Doakes as they began to leave the pier.

"I know a very nice spot serving native specialties. But let's do hurry. I don't want to miss this afternoon's steel band concert at the hotel."

They had gone only a few steps when they passed a stooped, rather frail black woman bending over a small gunnysack. The yellow ribbon in her hair contrasted starkly with the gray drabness of her attire. As she was placing three small fishes in the coarse burlap, a young black man came up behind her. The menacing sound of his voice as he addressed the old woman surprised the Spearmans and Mrs. Doakes. The young man was the hotel waiter, Vernon Harbley, whom they had noticed earlier.

"Mamie, I hear you been talkin' to the police about business that don't concern you." He stood a full foot taller than the recipient of his bullying, and his face showed the stress of restrained wrath. "You better jus' keep your mouth closed if Inspector Vincent comes 'roun again askin' about Ricky."

Mamie LeMans picked up her bag and backed away from her adversary. The Spearmans thought they detected a slight look of fear on her face, but she said nothing and hurriedly left the dock.

After a lunch in Cruz Bay, the Spearmans returned to the Plantation. They just missed being caught in one of the rainstorms that come up so suddenly in the Caribbean. The breeze from the storm cooled their room pleasantly, and, feeling tired from their exertions of the morning, they decided to nap.

Awakening later in the afternoon, Henry Spearman decided that he had time either to catch part of the afternoon concert or to take a hike before dinner. Still feeling the effects of the coucou that Mrs. Doakes had urged upon him at lunch, he opted for the hike. Spearman changed into his bermudas, which, because of his shortness, seemed to go to midcalf. This particular day he decided again to travel the Hawksnest Point trail. It always stimulated his appetite, which was becoming somewhat jaded after partaking for several days of the hotel's rich and abundant cuisine.

The trail was unusually quiet that afternoon. Even the chirping of the birds seemed to have been stilled. The only noticeable sounds were the occasional scratching noises of the hermit crabs and the rustling of leaves caused by scurrying lizards.

The quiet was suddenly broken. Professor Spearman was startled by the sound of something coming up behind him. Within the silence of the afternoon, the sounds seemed to echo in Spearman's ears, and the thought crossed his mind that he was threatened by some ominous and undefined danger along the trail in back of him. Spearman had seldom felt fear in his life but he felt it now. He whirled around and saw the figure of Justice Foote approaching him. A feeling of relief swept over him, and he stepped off the trail to let the famous jurist pass. As Foote breezed by, Spearman chided himself for his anxiety.

Then resuming his pace he walked until he reached the largest kapok tree on the path. There it was his habit to pause, for at this point one could just begin to hear the hollow *shooshing* sound of the blowpipe.

But this afternoon Spearman listened and heard nothing. Puzzled, he proceeded along the trail in the direction of the unique rock formation. Even as he was almost upon it, he failed to hear the sound. Curious as ever, he proceeded to investigate.

Peering over the margin, and directly into the wedge-like fault, he was surprised to see an object lodged at the base of the aperture where the waves pounded against the rock. At first, he could not make out what it was, and he thought that possibly a boulder had broken loose and become wedged in the pipe. But he soon realized that interpretation was an optimistic error; for the brutal truth was that the object lodged in the blowpipe was the body of the distinguished jogger who had passed Spearman only minutes before.

12

SATURDAY NIGHT was a special occasion at Cinnamon
Bay Plantation. The bar did little business then, for the
manager of the hotel hosted all of the guests at an elaborate party atop the ruins of the old sugar mill, which had
been converted into an open air pavilion. A large, conical
roof was positioned on supporting pillars in the center
of the pavilion so that visitors were afforded an unob-
structed view in all directions of the grounds, bays, and
nearby mountains.

As soon as a guest walked up the ramp to the pavilion,
he was greeted by the manager and his wife and invited to
imbibe the hotel's specialty, planter's punch (which was
available in copious quantities), and to partake at an
hors d'oeuvres table set with steaming platters of scallops
and shrimp entwined in bacon and barbecued meatballs
wrapped in grape leaves. Normally one of the highlights
of the party was the background music provided by a steel
band imported from Cruz Bay. However, this particular
evening the steel band was absent. And the atmosphere
was tenser than on the night when Bethuel Fitzhugh's
drowning was discussed. A drowning was an accident; but
this was murder.

Understandably the tenor of much of the conversation that evening went as follows:

"I'll bet his wife is not the usual mourning widow."

"Why do you say that?"

"Because they have been fighting like tigers ever since they arrived."

"The police think he was killed by a black, or a group of blacks, maybe even the same group involved in the St. Croix business."

"Now Harold, they don't know that for certain. That's only speculation."

"Maybe so, but given Foote's views on the blacks, I would say it is very sound speculation."

"I had heard that even the waiters here were quite unpleasant to him."

"In fact, some of them are being interrogated by the police right now."

"Well, the whole business we find rather frightening. We're checking out tomorrow."

"If the police will let you leave!"

"They say that little man over there is the one who discovered the body." A speaker pointed in the direction of Professor Spearman.

"I heard that he had seen Foote only moments before," another guest offered in a loud whisper.

Spearman felt uncomfortable. For one thing, he did not like being the focal point of so much conversation. For another, he had been horrified to learn that the death was not an accident. A preliminary autopsy had already revealed that the mortal wound resulted from a savage blow to the occipital area of the skull, administered by a blunt instrument. Moreover, Spearman was tired from the police interrogation that followed after he reported finding Foote's body. But he pretended not to be unduly upset, because he did not want his own emotions to further affect Pidge, who was already disconcerted.

Spearman decided the only way he could take his mind off the tragic events was to try to turn his attention elsewhere. He knew Pidge would be at ease if she thought her husband was engaging in his favorite preoccupation: observing the consumption behavior of his fellow guests. He also knew this was the one activity which could divert his attention. For to Spearman, as he reiterated over and again to his classes, this was what economics was all about. Had not the great Cambridge economist Alfred Marshall himself defined the subject as "the study of man in the ordinary business of life"? And had not this description been the mainstay of the greatest work done in the field? Spearman took this definition seriously even though it was considered a bit old-fashioned to some of his younger colleagues who saw economics as a solving of abstract puzzles unrelated to real events.

Spearman was observing one couple wolfing down free meatballs. He watched them consume until they reached the point of satiation. Then he directed his gaze elsewhere.

The behavior of Professor Matthew Dyke at this point captured his attention. For Dyke was not his usual self. He seemed much more serious, even brooding. Spearman watched him with interest as Dyke nursed a mug of planter's punch. He continued observing him for some time before Dyke noticed his faculty colleague and began to approach him.

"Someone on the island apparently understands the importance of applying my ethical theory, wouldn't you agree?"

"Whoever it is, my own hope is that the murderer is quickly apprehended and brought to justice," Spearman replied.

"But don't you see," Dyke said with intensity, "your so-called murderer is the person who in this case enacted justice. He is a genuine altruist."

"Why do you say 'he'? Has the sex of the killer been ascertained?"

"Well, man or woman, whoever it was is a benefactor of the human race."

Professor Spearman's wife, who had been chatting with some guests she had befriended, came over to him at this point with a look of grave concern. "Henry, may I speak to you for a moment?" Stepping aside she said to him, "I have just been talking with the Mullenses, you know, Harold and Cynthia, and they think that the drowning of that southerner—what was his name, Fitzhugh?—is related to the murders."

Looking up with a start, Spearman asked, "Why do they think that?"

"They claim that the drowning was no accident. Mr. Fitzhugh had antagonized a number of the help and, just like Foote and Decker, was probably marked for elimination." She added, "There could be further racial trouble. Do you think we should leave earlier than we had planned?"

Her husband replied, "Pidge, I have particular reasons for wanting to stay around here for awhile."

Inspector Vincent had tried to proceed in an orderly manner. He had first questioned the professor who found the corpse. But he could deduce no motive that Spearman might have for the crime. Also, Spearman was the person who reported the incident, though Vincent remembered that this was sometimes a clever diverting tactic used by the actual perpetrators of crimes. Vincent also doubted whether a person of such diminutive stature could deliver a blow of the type which the autopsy revealed had killed Justice Foote. Still, the first conversation he had with Spearman at the police station persuaded him that this professor was, as he put it, somewhat looney. And therefore he could not be completely dismissed as a suspect.

Vincent returned early the next morning to that portion of the trail along the blowpipe in hopes of finding some evidence which might point to the killer. Beginning with the trail itself, he scoured those parts on either side of the blowpipe. After some time he had covered about fifty feet of the path in each direction but had found nothing helpful. Then he began the much more difficult task of searching the rocky and wooded areas lining the trail.

Police work, contrary to the impression given by detective novels, is not glamorous. Indeed, the tedium of sifting for clues among dirt, leaves, rocks and bugs in the tropical heat would tax the most patient and durable of investigators. To be truthful the task was boring, and Vincent found himself wishing that the murder victim had not resigned from the Court so soon before his visit to St. John. If Foote had still been on the bench, the F.B.I., and not the Cruz Bay police force, would have had jurisdiction, and Vincent could have devoted his full energies to the Decker investigation, which involved working in more agreeable surroundings. But he pressed on. He had completed covering the terrain on the outside of the trail, and it was as he examined the ground below a large boulder just inside the path that he found his first clue. A red object almost hidden among some fallen bay rum leaves caught his eye. Stooping over he picked up what turned out to be a small axe. The hatchet had a red handle and, judging from the absence of any rust on its blade, Vincent knew that it had been left behind only recently. He tried to hold the implement by its end so as not to disturb any finger prints on the handle or any information that the blade might reveal under laboratory scrutiny. Gingerly turning it over he noticed that two initials had been carved into the butt end. The inspector surveyed his memory for names that matched the imprint on the axe. He could think of only one person whose name fitted those letters. He took a stubby pencil from his shirt pocket and made notes of his observations, taking care to describe the exact location of the object he had retrieved. Finishing this, he knew what his next order of business must be. He would return to Cinnamon and seek out the husky woman whose odd behavior at the hotel on a previous evening had not gone unnoticed by him.

"Tell Mr. Wyatt I need to see him for a moment." Inspector Vincent stood before the hotel's front desk and

tried to appear patient while the desk clerk rang the manager's office on the intercom.

"The police are here to see Mr. Wyatt."

"Just a minute, I'll see if he's free." Vincent heard the
intercom crackle back. Then the manager's secretary instructed the clerk to send the detective up. The offices for
the hotel were on a second floor, set back and over the
dining pavilion. One got to them by ascending a set of
stairs just off the lobby. Wyatt's office was in the front,
which gave him a view of the hotel's dock and main
beach. Vincent nodded to the secretary as she motioned
that he could go on in.

"I think you should know before I proceed any further
with my investigation that one of your guests has become
a prime suspect in the death of Justice Foote. I feel I must
interrogate her quite thoroughly and might have to make
an arrest."

Walter Wyatt visibly squirmed in his desk chair. The
hotel management school at Cornell had not prepared
him for such delicate situations. He knew that the hotel's
image required a quick solution to a publicized crime. On
the other hand it was clear to him that a false charge
against one of his guests could have disastrous consequences.

"I need hardly impress upon you, Franklin, the importance of your being absolutely certain about this. This
nasty business has already hurt the hotel's reputation and
we want to avoid any further disruption of our operation."
He got up from his chair and went to the window. "Look!
It is a beautiful day, and the main beach is practically
empty."

"I'm not interested in frightening or harassing your guests. But the evidence implicating Laura Burk is too strong to ignore." Vincent watched Walter Wyatt pace back and forth in front of the office window.

"I have just found what is probably the weapon used to kill Foote, only twenty feet or so from the murder site. It happens to be a hatchet with two initials on it: L.B." The inspector paused. "Laura Burk."

Wyatt seemed unimpressed with this argument. "Surely there must be many people with the initials L.B.," he protested.

"But not who discussed Justice Foote's jogging schedule with him just prior to his murder! I overheard such a conversation about five days before his death. I couldn't catch all of it but I did distinctly hear Foote tell this woman that he jogged every day on Hawksnest. And let me tell you something, that conversation between Miss Burk and Foote caused quite a row between the Justice and his wife after Laura Burk left. There might have been something between that woman and the Justice. At least Mrs. Foote certainly must have thought so. I know you keep a profile of your guests and I'd like to see what you have on Miss Burk."

Wyatt returned to his desk and buzzed his secretary. "Bring me the register for Laura Burk." The two men waited a few moments until the folder was placed on the manager's desk by a businesslike woman who passed in and out of the office without saying a word. "Thank you, Mrs. Monfrey," Wyatt said as the door closed behind her.

"Well I want to be cooperative, so here it is." Wyatt pointed to the file which the detective had requested and indicated that he would leave his office to allow Vincent to inspect the file undisturbed.

After Wyatt had left, the police officer seated himself behind the white wicker desk and put his pad and pencil upon the glass panel which served as its top. He opened the file and drew out a card which read as follows:

Name: BURK, Laura (Miss)
Street: 3615 Albermarle, N.W.
City: Washington, D.C.
Room Number: 26, Scott Beach
Arrival: 12/28, 4 PM
Business Address: Midlothian Institute, Federal Triangle,
        Washington, D.C. 20580
General References: Capital National Bank
        American Express
Activities: hiking, snorkeling
Health: No feathered pillows
Remarks: wants to be left alone; prefers company of older
        men
Prior Registrations: 6/71
Travel Agent: Potomac Travel, D.C. 20565
Current Stay: 12/21—open
Disposition of Bill: Pay Upon Departure.

The only entry on the card which seemed significant to Vincent during his initial perusal was that Laura Burk was from Washington, D.C., the home of Justice Foote. He also copied into his notebook the information that she preferred older men and was a loner in terms of the hotel's activities. "Older men," he thought to himself; "would that include Justice Foote?" He wouldn't put Foote in that category but a younger person might. Could

it be that Miss Burk was somehow involved with the former judge? Did this relationship begin before they came
to Cinnamon Bay? The police officer studied the card
again. For the first time in his investigation he began to
wonder about Virginia Pettingill Foote. Vincent had
never taken seriously the chatter about the Foote's domestic squabbles. Husbands and wives, he knew, sometimes could kill one another. But this was usually in the
heat of an argument, not in the premeditated fashion in
which Foote had apparently lost his life. But a jealous
wife, angered by an unfaithful husband, was another matter. Such a woman was quite capable of the most cold-
blooded deeds. And what could be more vindictive than
to pin the death on the third member of the triangle by
conveniently leaving a murder weapon with the initials
of that party inscribed on it? Vincent sat back and relaxed. He was pleased with himself and his train of reasoning. He had come up with not one but two possible
explanations for the death of Justice Foote. He had no
definitive proof, of course, but the circumstances certainly
seemed to merit a close interrogation of both women.

Still, neither of these candidates appeared implicated
in the death of General Decker. And Vincent had two
murders to solve, not one. It had seemed to him that the
two were related. He did not know this for certain, but the
Cinnamon Bay Plantation, to understate it, was an unlikely place for a murder. And *two* murders so close together: could that be by coincidence? He then reminded
himself of how both Foote and Decker had been TAR-
GETs in LeMans's *Raider* and how LeMans had been absent on the day of Foote's death. These thoughts seemed
to make up his mind. He would question Laura Burk and

Virginia Pettingill Foote and see if their answers were convincing. If they could persuade him of their innocence, his next move would be directed at Ricky LeMans and his ally Vernon Harbley.

As an afterthought before he left he scanned the rest of the contents of Miss Burk's folder. In addition to the registration card, it contained a number of sales vouchers recording the purchases which had been charged to her account thus far at the hotel. "Suntan lotion, postcards, a sandwich, a boat trip to St. Thomas, mostly drinks at the bar," he murmured to himself as he read through the chits. Nothing of any interest there, he decided. Then he set out to find Laura Burk.

Inspector Vincent proceeded to the bus pause to take a minibus to the Scott Beach area where Miss Burk was lodged. He had to wait only a few minutes before he was on his way. But as the vehicle headed north past the sugar mill ruins, he found that he would not have to go to Scott Beach to find Miss Burk after all. Situated just to the east of the road at that point was the hotel's bank of tennis courts and among those waiting for a match was none other than the object of his present pursuit.

He stepped off the slow-moving bus and ambled over to the tennis shelter, which was alongside the courts. Laura Burk was seated in one of the canvas folding chairs in front of the shingled, open-air structure. She was wearing the traditional tennis whites which at Cinnamon were socially obligatory. Her attire contrasted with the dark tan of her skin in a most complimentary way.

"Miss Burk, I hate to bother you but there is a matter of some urgency which I feel must be disposed of." He looked at her eyes. Was it his imagination or did she seem unusually calm for someone approached by an officer of the law? Vincent believed that surprise was the best method with which to approach a suspect. And so without any further word he asked her, "I have found a hatchet which is about to be examined by the police laboratory. If it is yours, and I believe the fingerprints will show that it is, there will be no point in your denying it." He watched carefully for her reaction.

Laura Burk seemed to compose her words in her mind and then spoke them calmly. "Why, thank you, officer! I didn't know I had lost one of my tools. But if you've found a hatchet with my initials on it, there's no need for fingerprinting. I'm sure it is mine. But really now," she said looking up at Vincent inquiringly, "I don't see what's all so urgent about the matter."

"What do you mean, one of your tools?" he said as he drew up another chair directly in front of her.

"Why, for my research."

"Just what kind of research does one do with a lethal weapon that turns up at the scene of a slaying?"

"What, you found my . . . Oh! Of course. I must have lost my hatchet up on Hawksnest trail when I had to leave hurriedly. I thought someone was coming. And the hatchet would have been right around the blowpipe someplace. But you don't think that I . . . ?"

"If the axe is yours," Vincent interrupted, "then I'm afraid I do. Unless you can explain what it was doing on the trail."

"I left it behind when I was up there searching for the petroglyphs."

"The petrowhats?"

"The petroglyphs. You know, the Carib Indian signs

carved into the rocks. As you're probably aware, they have long been known to exist up in the mountains of St. John. I had a theory there must be others like them on this side of the island."

The expression of incredulity on Franklin Vincent's face caused Laura Burk to draw up short. "Perhaps I should go back and explain. I am an archeologist. That you can check out with the Midlothian Institute in Washington. My boss, Dr. Dietrich Odendorf, will be able to confirm all this. Anyway, if I could prove my theory, it would establish conclusively the origin and meaning of these symbols. That would be a breakthrough in establishing the anthropological history of the West Indies. But my work has had to be in secret because I didn't want other archeologists to beat me to the punch and get in print first. Since I knew that Foote did a lot of hiking around the island, I decided to ask him whether he had ever noticed any such rock carvings. I even showed him a photograph of one taken at Camelberg Peak, and he told me that he had indeed seen something like it and had noted the fact in a log that he kept. He said he would show me the entry since it indicated the precise place where he remembered seeing it. We made arrangements to meet after breakfast the next day, and he brought his log with the drawing he had made. It seemed possible that it depicted one of the signs I had been searching for. He told me that he had found it carved on a boulder on Hawksnest trail, just past a large kapok tree near the blowpipe."

Laura Burk then made a sketch of the carving for the detective in his notebook. Franklin Vincent recognized the symbol as one he had seen a number of times in the mountainous region of St. John. But to him the

sign had come to have a much more sinister connotation. It was the chosen emblem of the islands' black
power movement.

He was now uncertain what to make of it all. He asked
Miss Burk to spell the name Odendorf, which he jotted in
his notebook on the page where he had made his earlier
entries from the hotel's file card. What Miss Burk had said
seemed to be possible, but to be truthful, Vincent dis-
trusted professional women. They never seemed to hold
him in the same regard that he had come to expect from
the women he had grown up with. Those he met from the
continent often made him feel awkward.

In the Virgin Islands, at least until recent years,
women stayed at home with their families. If they did any
outside work, they were employed as domestics or clerks.
With women like these, he felt comfortable. Their behavior was predictable. But the Laura Burks of the world
caused him to be anxious because they played so many
roles which traditionally had been assigned only to men.
He was on the verge of asking Miss Burk about the altercation he had witnessed between the Footes that seemed
to have been provoked by her presence at their table
when a man of about fifty came up behind Laura and
called out: "It's one o'clock! Time for our match."

Vincent watched as Laura Burk got up from her chair
and turned to acknowledge the greeting from the man
who was obviously her tennis date. "Have we finished our
interview, Inspector? I do have a previous engagement
with this gentleman."

"Just one more question, Miss Burk." Laura Burk
turned to her companion and suggested that he take the
court that they had reserved and she would join him in a

moment. And then she turned back to Vincent expectantly.

"Is it possible that your relationship with Justice Foote went well beyond the passing one you just told me about? In fact, your relationship with him went so far beyond the one you described that it caused great conflict in Foote's marriage."

Laura Burk laughed. "That's pure fantasy. As I said, I hardly knew the man. If you're implying that Foote's wife is jealous of me, I suggest that is a matter for you to take up with her. And now, Inspector, if you will excuse me, I am going to join my friend on the court."

"That's all for now. But I will have to ask you to remain at Cinnamon Bay until this matter is cleared up."

It was already early afternoon, and Vincent was hungry. He had been up earlier than usual that morning, and his investigation on the trail had taxed him more than his normal routine. Since he planned to question Mrs. Foote that same day, he decided not to go back to Cruz Bay where he normally ate but rather to take his lunch at the hotel. That prospect pleased him and not only because of his hunger. The luncheon buffet at the famed resort was always exciting to see, with its fresh melons, a variety of fruit and meat salads, a wide selection of Dutch and other continental cheeses, and even a selection of hot dishes. He rose from his chair at the tennis shelter and set out for the dining area. It was just a quick walk from the courts, and due to the lateness of the hour, the queue at the buffet was very short. The detective examined each platter and made his selections in a deliberate fashion.

His plate filled, he reconnoitered the room, finally selecting a table which faced the water in a rather vacant part of the dining area. As much as he looked forward to the cornucopia in front of him, Vincent nevertheless felt ill at ease. He was sure that some of the guests did not appreciate his presence there, and not only because he was a police officer. Though he was a native of the island, he had the distinct feeling of being viewed as an outsider when he partook of the hotel's pleasures.

Therefore he was surprised when he heard a voice behind him say, "May we join you for lunch?" Inspector Vincent turned around in his chair to see the couple who had now come up beside him: Dr. and Mrs. Clark. The request to sit with him had been totally unexpected, and he was relieved to have company since he felt even more conspicuous eating alone. He was particularly gratified that his fellow diners were the Clarks. Of all the hotel guests he had met in connection with these cases, the Clarks were the easiest to be with, as far as he was concerned. He attributed that to their midwestern backgrounds, which seemed to produce people who were less impressed with title and position than those who came to the islands from the Eastern Seaboard. For example, Mrs. Clark made no pretensions at being a professional woman. She was unabashedly a housewife.

Vincent suspected that easterners, at least the intellectuals and those who put on airs, were actually jealous of people like this. It was his experience that they could even make up malicious tales about them. He was not sure why they would do such a thing but it might be that a snobbish person realizes at bottom that his personality is not genuine, since his cues come from without and not from within.

"I hope you don't mind our asking to join you. We saw

you sitting here alone and thought you might like company," Judy Clark said.

"Judy, the Inspector may not remember us. This is my wife Judy Clark and I'm Doug Clark." Inspector Vincent rose halfway in his chair, holding his napkin with one hand while he drew out a chair for Mrs. Clark with the other.

"Yes, I remember you. Dr. and Mrs. Clark." He was thankful that they too had piled their plates high with food so his own helpings did not seem disproportionate.

"You must be terribly busy now, Inspector," Judy said to him. "We've heard about the second murder that was committed. Were you able to catch the person who killed the first man?"

"I'm sure the Inspector doesn't want our questions while he is eating lunch."

"Oh, I don't mind at all, really," Vincent said. "Unfortunately I must report that both murders are unsolved. But I am following a number of leads. Beyond that, I'm afraid there's very little else I can say."

The conversation then turned to more mundane things: the weather, the Clarks' children, and changes Franklin Vincent had observed in the islands in recent years. But before the lunch was finished, Vincent had an idea. He decided to ask the Clarks what they thought of some of the guests with whom he had talked.

"Do you mind if I ask you for some personal impressions? I hope I don't embarrass you by telling you that your judgment would carry great weight with me."

"Why, we'd be happy to help in any way we can." Dr. Clark replied for both of them.

The detective then proceeded to ask about Laura

Burk, Felicia Doakes, Jay Pruitt, and Matthew Dyke. Their responses contained no surprises. Although they knew Doakes and Pruitt personally, their knowledge of Laura Burk and Professor Dyke was minimal. Vincent wondered whether to bring up Ricky LeMans and Vernon Harbley but decided against it because it was unlikely they knew anything about them that he did not know already. He did, however, ask about their reaction to Virginia Pettingill Foote and had confirmed once again the strained nature of her relationship with her late husband. Almost as an afterthought he asked about Professor Spearman. And somewhat to his surprise he found that they considered the Spearmans their favorites among all the guests.

"Thanks for sharing your impressions with me. And I certainly enjoyed your company for lunch." Inspector Vincent excused himself and headed in the direction of the cottage occupied by Virginia Pettingill Foote. It was walking distance from the dining area and was situated on Cinnamon Beach, the largest of the several beaches at the hotel.

There was a mystique that had grown up about Cinnamon Beach among certain of the regular guests. It was their contention that the sand there had a softness that made it superior to that of the other beaches. Its texture was somewhere between refined and powdered sugar and was a delight to walk upon. Inspector Vincent, in his socks and sandals, was oblivious to the alleged appeal of the Cinnamon Beach. For him the beach route was simply the easiest way to his destination. He walked the hundred yards to the Foote cottage in short order and knocked firmly on the beachfront door.

"One moment!" he heard Mrs. Foote exclaim in response to his knock. Then, after a few seconds, the door was opened. Virginia Pettingill Foote stood in the doorway looking serene and confident wearing a white-on-white dressing gown which was neatly belted at the waist. Franklin Vincent introduced himself and showed his credentials.

"I was wondering when you would be around to question me. I understand I am not to leave the island until this formality is completed. But as I informed your office I must leave tomorrow. My husband's remains are being shipped to the States then, and I intend to accompany the casket."

"The questions I want to ask should not take long, Mrs. Foote. May I come in, or would you feel more comfortable if we went to the station at Cruz Bay?"

"Please come in. I want to get this over with as quickly as possible. As you can imagine I am still somewhat in a state of shock."

"Quite understandable. You have my deepest sympathies." He followed her into the parlor of the cottage suite and took the seat into which she motioned him. She sat across from him on a wicker sofa and waited expectantly for the questioning to begin.

"Mrs. Foote, is there any reason you can think of why someone would want to kill your husband? That is, did he have any enemies, perhaps personal enemies or someone who was seeking revenge because of something your husband did?"

"Did my husband have enemies?" Her tone was one of sarcastic understatement. "Liberals, socialists, members of minority groups, Marxists: one thing they all shared in common was a hatred for my husband. You must know he was a controversial figure—both in the Senate and then on the Court. Many people violently disagreed with him. And I suppose it is possible that any number of his political and legal opponents might go so far as to murder him."

"But do you know of any one person who was the most likely to do this? Did your husband ever talk about such a person? Perhaps even receive a threatening letter or a phone call?"

"My husband received a great number of abusive letters. But he used to dismiss them as the work of harmless cranks."

"Is there anyone at the hotel with whom your husband could have had an argument recently?" Inspector Vincent took out his notepad and pencil as Mrs. Foote recounted the altercation which her husband had had with Ricky LeMans shortly after their arrival at Cinnamon Bay. She explained how the Justice had gone up to the bandleader upon finding himself displayed as the TARGET in that issue of LeMans's *Raider*. He had told her afterwards how LeMans had threatened him, and Virginia recalled how her husband seemed unusually angered by the episode.

"That's very useful, Mrs. Foote," Vincent responded, obviously pleased at securing this information. "Is there anything you can recall about your husband's relations with anyone else at the hotel?"

"No, but that should not be too surprising. Even if there were other incidents, he would not necessarily tell me about them. My husband and I had little in common, and sometimes days would go by without our discussing anything of consequence. He was, in fact, a secretive person in his private life, confiding his thoughts and observations only to his diary. Not that I minded. I can be frank with you, Inspector, and tell you something you have probably heard from others anyway. My husband and I had incompatible personalities. His side interests were in athletics; mine are in art and theater—not that I am opposed to sports. In fact I enjoy sailing and horseback riding. But my husband detested these activities—considered them to be the pastimes of the rich and idle. Oh, you see, Inspector, he married 'up' as they say, and people who do this can seldom feel at ease in their spouse's circles. All of my friends and family tried to make him feel welcome—went out of their way to do so, even when he was abrasive to them. But he claimed they resented him and imagined all sorts of slights."

"What sort of slights seemed to offend him?"

"Oh, they were imaginary, as I said. But Curtis thought his being a senator and an athlete would have accorded him unusual respect. He never understood that his political position and the he-man image only appeared unseemly in my circle of friends. Because of his touchiness, we largely went our separate ways. I have no doubt he had acquaintances about whom I knew nothing."

"Do you think that perhaps Miss Laura Burk was one of these?"

"Oh, you mean Miss 'Candid Camera'? I see you already know how she was chasing after Curtis. It was all that obvious wasn't it? She is an original, that one. His other trysts were through ruses that were not so imaginative. But to pose as an archeologist is unique. There was one once—oh, she wasn't as subtle, of course—who pretended she had to meet Curtis because she was writing a thesis on his legal opinions—claimed to be comparing them to Justice Marshall's. Ha! But an archeologist, that's clever.

"You won't believe this, Inspector, but she actually had the *nerve* to come to our table at dinner, and in front of me, plan a rendevous with my husband on the pretense of discussing some rock carving she had photographed. I don't mind them having a liaison, but triangles should be formed discreetly. One would think my husband, of all people, could be judicious about such matters."

Inspector Vincent rose from the couch and walked over to the window louvres. He had not expected a newly widowed woman to be so frank about the shortcomings of her spouse. "Did you see the photograph yourself, Mrs. Foote?"

"Why yes, of course. She left the picture with us that night. I glanced over it, and it appeared authentic enough—very primitive and all that. They claimed it was an Indian carving. She even pretended to be with the Midlothian! I really have to laugh when I think of them out there in the woods making that silly carving on a rock."

"You say your husband met with this woman after breakfast the very next morning."

"That's right."

"Do you know what went on in that meeting?"

"Well, I can't give you the intimate details but I can tell you the pretext of the meeting. Curtis claimed that he had seen a carving similar to the one depicted in the photograph during one of his trail runs. My husband kept a log of all his daily activities and observations—

and I mean all of them; he was very fastidious about this—and so he simply invited her to meet with him to compare his notes on what he had seen with what she was looking for."

"Did your husband say anything about this meeting? Did he indicate whether the notes in his diary matched the photograph?" asked Vincent.

"You don't suppose I showed any interest in that, do you? After the episode at dinner, I was not going to lend dignity to their charade. But the picture is still here—and there's his log on the dresser." Virginia Foote pointed to the bureau on the other side of the room.

"I'm afraid I will have to take them with me, Mrs. Foote. It may contain important evidence but it will be returned to you."

"Oh, keep it as long as you like, Inspector. In fact, you may need it quite awhile. My husband was a very vain man, and he considered even his most vagrant thought worth recording for posterity."

Inspector Vincent located the photograph and log on the dresser and turned back to the Justice's wife. "Mrs. Foote, I know you will understand the necessity of my asking this. You yourself have indicated that you did not have an ideal marriage. I must ask you where you were the afternoon your husband was murdered?"

"I'm afraid I don't have what you would call a good alibi. I saw Curtis leave our room around four p.m., and I remained here alone until the police came with the news of his death."

Inspector Vincent raised his eyebrows. "You're right, Mrs. Foote, that isn't much of an alibi. But I have no grounds for detaining you and you're free to leave the island tomorrow if you like." The police detective excused himself and stepped into the sultry tropic afternoon.

Sultry tropic afternoons were not to the liking of the Spearmans. During this time of day they normally stayed in their cottage. That afternoon Pidge was writing post-cards and Henry was finishing Douglas Day's biography of Malcolm Lowry. Spearman's professional commitments kept him from reading widely outside of economics, but on his vacations he did try to become acquainted with the writings of some of the winners of that year's National Book Awards.

"Did you like the book?" Pidge Spearman asked, look-ing up from her writing table.

Her husband, who was lying on the bed, had just closed the volume and placed it on the nightstand next to him. "Lowry led a troubled life, Pidge, which ended in a tragic death. But I think I felt most sorry for those he married. It could not have been easy to live with such a high-strung individual."

"His married life sounds like the Footes'! But in their case it seems to be the wife who is hard to live with."

"Oh, you'd have to read the book to see how terribly unpleasant a marriage can be. I don't think there's any comparison between living with a Malcolm Lowry and living with a Virginia Foote. In the case of the Lowrys there was sometimes physical violence."

"Well remember that many people around here don't put physical violence beyond Mrs. Foote. Anybody who shows such malice towards her husband—there's no tell-ing what she would do if she had the chance."

Spearman had heard this gossip about Mrs. Foote. And having observed how acrimonious their relationship could be he himself had pondered the question as to whether she may have been guilty of killing her spouse. But he was inclined to be skeptical of any wife being likely to kill her husband. This skepticism had nothing to do with any relative physical disadvantage wives might have in carrying out such a plan. Anybody, after all, could pull a trigger or administer a poison. His reservation was based on economics, specifically the theory of capital.

With divorce laws being rather liberal, and given the present structure of generous alimony payments, a woman usually would be financially far better off by divorcing her husband than by killing him. In most instances, the dollar amount of alimony payments over her expected lifetime would far exceed the death benefits of social security and insurance policies, which would accrue only if the murderer was not caught. The only difficulty with this was whether a woman as wealthy as Virginia Pettingill Foote would be influenced by these considerations. After all, the amount of money she could get in alimony would be relatively small compared to her income from other sources. Still, Spearman knew that there was no scientific reason to believe that an additional dollar to a rich person gave any less satisfaction than to someone who is poorer.

Spearman suddenly got up from the bed and began to pace. He was usually a jovial man but his mind was troubled. Perhaps it was because he had just finished such a distressing book. But as he examined his feelings he decided all of his melancholy was not traceable to the book he had just read. Since arriving at Cinnamon Bay with his wife, on what was to be a happy holiday, there had been two murders and a drowning. And he had been in the presence of Decker, Fitzhugh, and Foote only moments before their deaths. Perhaps that is why these events weighed so heavily on him. Could all of these unlikely incidents be unrelated? The drowning could be dismissed as a coincidence, but he knew the police suspected a link between the two murders. Spearman's training in statistics led his own thinking in that direction, too. Not that murders were random events, he thought, but if they had any randomness, two would not likely occur in such close proximity without some correlation with each other.

He was brought out of his reflections for a moment when his wife rose from the desk and said, "I want to send these postcards to the children before the afternoon mail goes out. Do you want to walk along with me?"

"No thank you, dear. I think I'll stay here. I do hope you sent the children my greetings and let them know I'm making good use of the snorkel mask." Her reassurance given, Pidge Spearman left her husband to his thoughts.

Alone in the cottage, Henry Spearman went into the bathroom and splashed some cool water on his face. He hoped to wash away the gloom that hung over him. But the water running into the basin reminded him for some inexplicable reason of the blowpipe. Then he realized that the sound of the water was similar to that of the rough surf climbing the walls of the rocky aperture where he had discovered the body of Justice Foote. He left the bathroom immediately and reentered the bedroom. The gloom was still there. As he stared out the louvred windows toward the road, a passing minibus came into his line of vision. How could he forget that this vehicle had been General Decker's last bus to Turtle Bay on that fateful night?

A shudder went through him; he turned sharply away and walked hurriedly to the beach side of the room and stared out at the sweep of white sand. Perhaps here his thoughts could turn to more pleasant matters.

But his hopes were dashed. In spite of the afternoon heat, his skin rose into goosebumps. The only object he saw on the beach that afternoon was an empty chaise longue.

Since there was no escaping thoughts of the morbid events of the last few days, Henry Spearman did the second best thing: he would channel his thinking about these matters toward more productive ends. The economist pulled out the chair in which his wife had been sitting and placed a piece of the hotel's stationery before him. Then he took a pen from the desk and poised it over the blank paper, which he contemplated for a few minutes.

This posture was not unfamiliar to those who knew his method in tackling a puzzling problem in economics. Unlike many of his younger colleagues, who did much of their work seated at a computer terminal, Spearman was old-fashioned enough to believe that the most intractable difficulties gave way to logical processes revealed through paper and pencil.

Soon he began to write. Earlier he had formulated a hypothesis as to who had killed General Decker. But his economic reasoning had not persuaded the police. Now he was organizing his thoughts on the assumption that the two murders were related. He wrote slowly in a crimped style, and as he set his pen back on the desk, his wife entered the cottage.

"Henry, I'm back!" But he motioned for silence as he studied the results in front of him. Mrs. Spearman watched her husband from across the room and knew that he was engrossed once again in his economics. But she would have been surprised to see that in this instance her husband's "economics" consisted of the following list:

Laura Burk
Dr. Douglas Clark
Judy Clark
Felicia Doakes
Matthew Dyke
Virginia Pettingill Foote
Vernon Harbley
Ricky LeMans
Jay Pruitt

Spearman scrutinized the names for a long span of time. He believed that among them was the killer of Justice Foote. The drowning of Bethuel Fitzhugh was probably an accident. But logic had led him tentatively to proceed as if the Decker and Foote murders were connected. Was economic reasoning consistent with this hypothesis? He went down the list in a methodical manner, concentrating on the question of who killed Curtis Foote. He was persuaded that economic analysis had eliminated Virginia Pettingill Foote as a likely suspect.

Only eight candidates remained.

13

FRANKLIN VINCENT entered the front door of the Cruz Bay police station. He had just returned from Cinnamon Bay Plantation with the intention of studying the large leather volume and the photograph he had procured from Mrs. Foote. As soon as he entered the building, the desk sergeant said to him, "Mr. Osborne up on Gallows Point called this morning. He says somebody stole his spinnaker last night—from right off his boat. He's hoppin' mad about it and wants us to get it back immediately."

"Naturally Osborne would expect it back right away," Vincent said testily. "Did you tell him it would help if he didn't leave expensive things on the deck of his yacht? At any rate you'll have to put Phil on it because I'm still working on the Cinnamon homicides." There was a sense in which Vincent would have happily taken the assignment to track down the missing sail. Such mundane crimes were his bread and butter. But in spite of himself he was intrigued by the hotel murders, murders which, if he could solve them, would give him more fame than Aberfield in St. Thomas had ever attained.

The inspector circled the front counter and walked into the small back room that served as his office. With his free hand he clicked on the light and settled himself at his desk. He glanced over the photograph, making a mental image of what was depicted there. When Vincent looked at the size of the volume in front of him he sighed. If Mrs. Foote were right about her husband's painstaking detail, this could be a long evening. Before getting comfortable he got up and turned on the floor fan in the corner of the room. The fan could not lower the temperature in the office, but the circulating air made Vincent feel cooler. He returned to the desk and drew his humidor closer to him. After filling his pipe—his first bowlful of the day, he reflected—the detective leaned back in his swivel chair and propped his feet on the desktop. The bulky volume rested on his lap as he opened the front cover and began searching for the date on which Foote had allegedly made the entry about the petroglyph. This seemed to be the appropriate starting point. If there were an entry about such a symbol written before his evening encounter with Laura Burk, this would tend to corroborate her story. Even so, he knew he would have to read the entire log. Franklin Vincent wanted to know if there were any record of Justice Foote having had contact with Laura Burk prior to their meeting at Cinnamon. He also felt that a close reading of the chronicle might reveal whether Foote had enemies whom he feared.

The smoke from the pipe slowly swirled behind his head as the fan gently churned the air in the room. At first it was not easy for him to follow the various entries. Not that the handwriting posed any problem: The Justice wrote in clear, bold strokes. Vincent's difficulty was with the style, since he had never known of anyone who wrote his own diary in the third person. Once he got used to the Justice's affectation, he soon found the section he was looking for. On January eighth, five days prior to the Justice's death, Curtis Foote had recorded the following entry: "Foote felt tired during afternoon jog on Hawksnest. Deviated from trail just past kapok tree to rest in shade. While steadying himself by gray boulder, he observed curious carving in shallow crevice. Reminiscent of primitive art forms he had seen in Arizona." Following this entry was Foote's attempt to replicate the design he had seen. Vincent recorded in his own notebook the page number and date of this entry.

This bit of corroboration of Laura Burk's tale led him to believe for the first time that her alibi probably held up. It appeared more and more to him that his orderly process of elimination was leading to the conclusion that LeMans and Harbley had acted together to commit the murders. Both were at the scene of the crime of the first homicide. They had in their *Raider* pinpointed the murdered men as TARGETs. And they were the only suspects with a motive for killing each of them, so far as he knew.

Nevertheless, he wanted to be sure that he had exhausted all possibilities before arresting the two men. So he pressed on with his reading to see if any and all accounts by the Justice of meetings with Laura Burk were consistent with her own rendition of the events to Vincent. It turned out that Miss Burk's stories squared in every detail with that told by the diary. From January ninth on, there were only two meetings noted: the first was at the hotel's nightclub when Vincent had been observing the activities of the guests; the second was the post-breakfast appointment the next day when Foote had presumably shown the January eighth entry to Miss Burk.

The inspector sat forward and knocked the ashes from

his pipe into the wastebasket. He set his darkened billiard down and picked up a pencil to record his thoughts. It appeared to him, based on this evidence, that Laura Burk's story might very well be credible, though he realized there was a possibility that all of the Justice's entries involving Miss Burk had been manufactured to conceal the real nature of their relationship.

Many of the entries recorded after the second Foote-Burk meeting were pertaining to Foote's personal matters. The final entry, although this could not have been known to Foote at the time, contained no momentous peroration: "Wrote Siegel to have all my robes cleaned."

Franklin Vincent riffled the papers of the log to the initial entry about the petroglyph. He decided that he would work backwards from this point specifically to see if there might be any other entries involving Miss Laura Burk or some other information which would cast any light on Foote's mysterious death.

Virginia Pettingill Foote had been right. The notes that made up only one day's observations often consumed as many as four pages of the hefty volume. The inspector twisted in his chair to get more comfortable. But he had not completed two days of entries before something made him sit bolt upright in his chair. He had only been hoping but not expecting to find evidence linking the death of Foote with that of General Decker. Yet there it was, in the stark, unmistakable hand of the judge himself: "The news that General Hudson Decker was poisoned last Friday was told Foote by his wife. It may be that what was seen on the terrace was of more import than Foote had imagined. Only problem: uncertain what *was* seen."

Vincent read and reread this amazing entry. What

could it mean? Did it imply that Curtis Foote knew who murdered General Decker? If so, that would give Decker's murderer a motive to kill Foote. But if Foote did have some information, why didn't he come to the police with it? Surely a former judge, of all people, would not obstruct justice by not reporting such an incident. Unless, of course, he was trying to protect someone. And that might explain why Virginia Pettingill Foote did not even mention her husband's knowledge of the Decker murder. Another visit to the widowed Mrs. Foote was clearly in order.

The young lady behind the desk was assisting Mrs. Foote in the paperwork associated with her planned departure the next morning. She was in the process of explaining the arrangements when she looked up and saw Franklin Vincent enter the room.

"Good evening, Mr. Vincent," she said cheerily, "is there something we can help you with?"

"When you are finished assisting Mrs. Foote, I'd like the opportunity to speak with her. Would that be all right, Mrs. Foote?" She turned in his direction and responded, "Finished with the diary already? There was no hurry. You could have sent it to me."

"I'm afraid I'm not ready to return the log as yet. But I do want to ask you about something I found in it."

"Of course, anything I can do to help you find my husband's murderer. I have just finished up here."

The two of them sat down at a coffee table in the hotel's lobby. Vincent spread the book before them with the pages turned to the entry which had caused his excitement earlier.

"Mrs. Foote, I would like you to read this statement of your husband and tell me what you make of it." Virginia Foote moved the heavy volume closer in front of her and began to read.

"Oh, yes, I'd forgotten all about that. I can certainly see why you would come back to inquire about it. Unfortunately there's even less here than meets the eye."

"Well, you just let me decide that. Right now I want to know what your husband meant by this statement." Vincent tried to be gentle with Mrs. Foote, who after all was a new widow, but he could not help the sharp edge that crept into his voice.

"When I tell you, you will understand what I meant when I said my husband recorded even his most vagrant thoughts and fleeting observations. Shortly after I told him an autopsy had revealed that General Decker had been poisoned, that seemed to set him off. He didn't know Decker personally, of course, but they both had their circles in Washington. Anyway, he began to imagine that he saw Decker murdered—not that he saw the man die or anything—but that he saw the poison administered. When he told me this, I asked him who did it. But he didn't know. He reminded me that a large crowd had been on the cocktail terrace that night. The steel band had been playing, the guests were drinking and chatting, and my husband had just asked me to dance. We were proceeding toward the bandstand when he apparently turned his head in the direction of General Decker's table. There was much milling about over there, and as he later recalled it, he couldn't see who did it, but he thought that a drink the waiter had just served to the General was tampered with. That brief sideways glance was enough for him to claim that he took in the sight of a hand dropping something into the glass a few seconds before the General drank from it. I told him that it was probably only the General's own hand pouring in some medication or other. But my husband was a hard man to convince. Of course, Inspector, you probably know all lawyers are detectives at heart—at least they think they can be detectives. My husband knew he had nothing for the police to go on, but he had such unbearable pride in his powers of observation that he was dumbfounded that he could not place a person with the event he thought he saw. Yet at the same time he hoped that he would see something later that would tie it all together. But he never did. At least he never said anything to me about it. And he'd have told me, Inspector. He wouldn't have missed the opportunity to say, 'I told you so!'"

"Did you or your husband discuss these suspicions with anybody else? Think before you answer; this could be very important."

"I don't have to think about it, because he told me not to tell anyone about the matter unless he became certain about what he saw that night. Of course, I had no intention of talking about it anyway, since I considered the whole thing inconsequential, a figment of his imagination. And I'm certain he wouldn't share such a speculation with others. My husband was too sensitive about his image to risk appearing foolish."

"Is it possible that anyone could have had access to your husband's log?"

"That's not likely. He always kept it among his personal things, and we locked the room whenever we left. That book was very precious to him. It was to be the basis of his memoirs. I think he would have known if anyone had disturbed it in his absence. Besides, what reason would anyone have for wanting to read the log—unless they already knew that my husband was suspicious about the Decker murder? But as I just told you, no one knew about that but me."

When she had finished with this statement, she was surprised at the look of resolve on Vincent's face. He stood up from his chair and announced to her, "Thank you, Mrs. Foote, you've been more than cooperative. I know I won't be troubling you anymore about this matter. In fact, I believe I can safely say that before the day ends those responsible for the murder of General Decker and your husband will be in custody."

Ricky LeMans and Vernon Harbley sat at the small wooden table in Mamie LeMans's house. Ricky's mother stood at the cast-iron stove preparing callalou soup for her son and his compatriot. She saw Ricky so seldom nowadays that she hid her true feelings about Vernon Harbley so as not to jeopardize the privilege of her house serving as their meeting place. As it was, Ricky came there rarely enough, but when he did visit, she never missed the opportunity to indulge him with home cooking.

"So when will the next issue appear?" Harbley asked.

"Thanks to Pelau, we've got the money to go ahead now—and for another two months. He brought us over four hundred bucks. I don't know what we'll do after that. So we've got to choose our TARGETs carefully. Do you have an idea who our next one should be?"

"The heat's on from Cinnamon. I think it better be somebody from one of the other islands," Harbley replied.

"Well, the heat's on in all the islands, according to Pelau. He's been only one step ahead of the police but thought he had shook them from his trail when he was here. The time I met with him, we took extra precautions, including getting him off the island on Vere's boat. Right now he's supposed to be in the Bahamas and said he didn't know when he could get back to help us."

"Well, if that's the case I think we should go after Mr. Osborne on Gallows Point."

"Osborne's OK, I guess. But I don't want to pick anybody at the hotel again for awhile. You're the only contact we have with Cinnamon now," LeMans said.

Mamie interrupted their strategy discussion by placing two bowls of hot soup before them. The mixture of salt beef, crabs, and dasheen leaves created a piquant aroma that filled the room. Vernon Harbley looked up at Ricky's mother and said, "You make the best callalou in all the islands." His demeanor towards Mrs. LeMans was far more subdued in the presence of her son than when he saw her on the dock a day ago. At that time he was carrying out a mission. Ricky LeMans had told Harbley to chastise his mother about talking with the police. And he had carried out his friend's instructions. But Harbley knew no son would ever want to be present when someone outside the family criticized his mother. Blood ties were too strong for that.

Suddenly Mamie looked up and appeared to be listening intently. "What's the matter, Mama?" Ricky asked when he saw the look of concentration on her face.

"There's someone comin' up the road and they done just turned in the drive and he's comin' up here."

"Are you expecting someone tonight? You know Vernon and I need to be alone."

"Who'd I be expectin' anyway?"

"I don't know, Mama, but get rid of 'em, and don't tell 'em I'm here." Mrs. LeMans went out on the porch of her ramshackle dwelling and watched for the approaching vehicle. Soon she was reflected in the headlights of a jeep which she realized belonged to the police. Franklin Vincent braked the car alongside the porch and clambered out.

"Good evening, Mamie, I see you've got company."

"No, I'm here alone."

"Then you wouldn't mind if I took a quick look around, would you? Maybe there's someone here you don't know about."

Mamie laughed nervously. "How could somebody be in my house without my knowin' it?"

"Maybe they're not in the house right now but I'm here to check on that."

"Now you just stay outside, Mr. Vincent."

"Mamie, we've always been friends. Are you going to let me in the house or do I have to use the search warrant I have with me?"

"You can come in, Vincent," Rickey LeMans said from the doorway behind his mother. "But if you've come to talk about those murders, we've already played that gig."

"I've just rescheduled you and a friend of yours for a return engagement. Do you know where I can find Vernon Harbley?" Harbley's appearance in the doorway answered the inspector's question. "There's no sense in our talking anymore, I've already told you everything I know."

"Well we'll find out about that at the station. I've got warrants for your arrest for the murder of Decker and Foote."

"On what grounds?" LeMans said, angrily indignant.

"We'll discuss the grounds and your rights at the station."

Mamie LeMans was visibly upset. She began to sob and then railed at her son, "What have you gone and done now? I begged you so many times to stay away from Vernon and just stick to your music."

"Don't worry, Mama, the police have nothin' on us. You just keep the soup warm. We'll be back tonight!"

Inspector Vincent was pleasantly surprised that LeMans and Harbley had accompanied him so peaceably. But their attitude of cockiness quickly withered at the station when they realized that they actually were being charged as co-conspirators in the murder of Hudson T. Decker and Curtis Foote and were about to be incarcerated for these crimes.

Franklin Vincent had decided even before picking them up that he would interrogate LeMans and Harbley separately. The detective was well aware from earlier encounters how the two could communicate silently with each other through a look or a gesture. And he wanted no collusion while trying to elicit a confession from them. While confident of his conclusions, Vincent knew his evidence was not yet terribly strong. Harbley had been the last person to be seen with Decker's poisoned drink. Le-Mans had openly threatened Justice Foote. Both men were jointly responsible for the TARGET selections. A jury should have no trouble putting these pieces together, he thought, but a pair of confessions would be so much more desirable and convenient.

Franklin Vincent did not get to sleep until five a.m. But it was to be the best sleep he'd had since his investigations had begun. Within the last hour Vincent had emerged triumphant from the interrogations. His strategy had worked; both Ricky LeMans and Vernon Harbley had confessed to the Cinnamon Bay murders.

14

THE NEWS OF THE CONFESSIONS of LeMans and Harbley lifted the pall that had enshrouded the hotel. Many of the guests did not want to show how concerned, even frightened, they had been by the tragic events that had taken place during their stay. But the glib facade they donned only served to accentuate the great feeling of relief they actually shared. That morning there was much good-natured banter as a number of the guests were gathering at the hotel's open-air foyer in front of the entrance to the dining room. This group was waiting for the arrival of the Park Service Ranger, who each week at this time conducted a nature walk in the Virgin Islands National Park adjoining the hotel's grounds.

Meeting that morning for the excursion was a larger crowd than usual, owing no doubt to the feeling of greater freedom the news of the jailings had brought. Among them were Mr. Jay Pruitt and his bride Pamela, Mrs. Felicia Doakes, the Spearmans, Professor Matthew Dyke, Harold and Cynthia Mullens, Dr. and Mrs. Douglas Clark, and Miss Laura Burk.

"I guess I'm no longer Public Enemy Number One!" Jay Pruitt chortled to no one in particular. He had seemed to relish being a suspect in the Decker homicide and did not want to relinquish his notoriety.

"Jay, please don't talk like that," his wife whispered. But he ignored her as he bounced from guest to guest to impress upon them the virile image which he thought attached to someone who could have been suspected in the murder of a famous general.

Pamela Pruitt would have been relieved to know that her husband's gaucheries went largely unobserved since almost everyone was intent on trying to learn the full story surrounding the murders and the capture of the confessed killers. Up to now, most of them possessed the bits and snippets that went with unverified rumors, and not the least of the reasons for choosing to join together in the nature walk was to afford an opportunity to become acquainted with the details.

Only Felicia Doakes's presence could have been confidently predicted by a historian of the hotel's activities schedule. She never missed an opportunity to explore the environs against the chance of finding some spice or herb or root which would enhance a recipe she was concocting. Her favorite quotation was from Brillat-Savarin: "The discovery of a new dish does more for the happiness of mankind than the discovery of a star."

Mrs. Doakes happened to be chatting with Dr. and Mrs. Clark. ". . . and if you see a little green fern with orange berries, be sure and call it to my attention. I've been hoping to spot one for weeks. The berries lend a pungency to any recipe calling for deep-sea fish." They stared at her blankly, finding it curious that she showed so little interest in learning the story of her cousin's death.

"I'm not very good at identifying plants. I was just terrible in biology. But if I see any orange berries, I'll holler and let you know," Judy Clark finally responded.

"Did the police come to tell you how they caught General Decker's murderer? After all, they owe you that much. You were his closest living relative." Douglas Clark seemed sympathetic.

"I told the police some time ago not to bother me about Hudson's murder. He's dead now, poor man. There's nothing that dwelling on the details can accomplish. Besides, I've always maintained that life is for the living. Hudson's number was up and the two men in jail were only the instruments of fate. Perhaps if he had taken my advice and not stayed in cottage thirteen. . . ."

"I can't agree with your superstition, Mrs. Doakes, but I must admit that in the case of General Decker a violent end might have been expected—although not the type he actually met with."

"What do you mean, Doug, not the type he actually met with?" his wife inquired.

"I mean, his being a military man and all."

"Well I'm sure, Dr. Clark, Hudson would have preferred to go on the battlefield. But fate usually doesn't give us our preferences in such matters. You're a medical man; surely you can appreciate that. Now as I was saying about those berries. . . ."

Cynthia and Harold Mullens, who were listening to this conversation, seemed impatient. They had joined Mrs. Doakes hoping to absorb information for future palaver. They could hardly contain their disappointment in her persistence in discussing the local flora. "Surely *someone* around here must care about how the police caught those two blacks and what they found out from them," Cynthia Mullens said to her husband.

Mrs. Doakes seemed pained at their attitude. "Really,

Mrs. Mullens, if that's *all* you're interested in, there's the man who seems to know." She pointed to Professor Matthew Dyke. At that the Mullenses immediately made toward the small group that circled the theologian.

Mrs. Doakes then turned back to the Clarks and said with an exasperated tone of voice, and still within earshot of the retreating Mullenses, "My word, this is supposed to be a nature walk, not a game of 'Clue.'"

Mr. and Mrs. Mullens inserted themselves between the Spearmans and Laura Burk, who were listening to Matthew Dyke. At that point he was saying, ". . . seems to clinch it, although in these instances justice would be better served if the murderer of Foote, at least, went unpunished."

"Well I certainly don't agree with that," Laura Burk objected. "I didn't know Curtis Foote very well, but in the few contacts we had, I was surprised at how different he was from his public image. I for one am delighted that the murderers have been caught."

Harold and Cynthia looked at each other. They were still convinced that the altercation between the Footes which followed Miss Burk's presence at the table that night proved Laura Burk and the Justice were more than just casual acquaintances. In fact, earlier that morning, when Virginia Pettingill Foote was departing on the boat with her husband's casket, Cynthia Mullens had remarked to Harold how tasteless it was for Laura Burk to be on the dock at the time.

"I'm afraid I don't have the energy to disabuse you of your views of Foote, since I was up all night trying to see that the rights of the two men were protected from abuse by a racist police force. If you will read my book you will see how the elimination of people like Foote can be ethically justifiable."

"And what about General Decker? You seem to forget that he was, as you say, 'eliminated' also by these two good samaritans," Laura Burk said testily.

Dyke stared at Miss Burk for a few moments forming his thoughts. "No, I possibly wouldn't include General Decker in Foote's category, but he must have done something to merit the enmity of the black community here or he would not have appeared in the TARGET."

Before Miss Burk could reply, Harold Mullens interjected, "Everyone seems to know what's going on around here but us. All we've heard is that two men have been jailed for committing the two murders. Have they actually confessed to the crimes?"

"I'm afraid they have," Dyke said, "and from what I can gather, without coercion. I tried to get in last night at the police station but was barred at the door. However, my contacts with the black community here provide me with reliable information. They feel I am one of the few whites on the island who have merited their trust. The two men in jail are LeMans, the bandleader, and Harbley, one of the waiters here at Cinnamon. I'm told they were picked up yesterday evening at LeMans's mother's house. They were brought to the police station, and before the night was out, both men had confessed and implicated the other."

Professor Spearman, who had been silently listening up to this point, asked a question: "Do you happen to know whether the two men were interrogated together or separately?"

"Oh, I was concerned about that too. They were questioned separately—in fact, when I got to Cruz Bay, the police had just finished interrogating LeMans, and I discovered that his confession was apparently given without physical coercion, at least it was not beaten out of him. I happened to see them taking Harbley into the room after they were finished with LeMans. The police were obviously taking precautions to keep the two from having any contact with each other. They kept Harbley for considerable time before he finally admitted that he and LeMans had killed Foote and Decker. My contacts tell me that, surprisingly, Harbley was not strong-armed either."

"How can you be so sure? I've heard that the police can use truncheons these days in a way that leaves no visible bruises," Pidge Spearman observed.

"I'm aware of that, but in this case an employee at the jail—I'm really not free to say who it is—has told me this."

"I assume that since they both confessed, they will get off more lightly than if they were found guilty as a result of a trial," Henry Spearman remarked.

"That's usually the case, but of course there's the possibility that they wouldn't be found guilty at all if they hadn't confessed."

"Well, what if one confessed and the other didn't?" Spearman queried.

"I don't know what they would do about that, but isn't that rather academic? After all, they both confessed."

"I suppose you may be right," Spearman acknowledged.

"In any event, Henry, now that they've caught those two, we can resume our vacation," Pidge entreated.

Mrs. Spearman's wishes seemed to be answered that

morning, for with the arrival of the Park Ranger, the attention of everyone in the group was diverted in his direction.

Professor Spearman sat motionless in the chair beside the desk. He had changed from his hiking garb of the morning into a pair of tan cotton shorts and a black pullover. It was early in the afternoon, and most of the guests were still lunching. But Spearman had skipped the noon meal, explaining to Pidge that he did not seem to have an appetite. She attributed his lack of hunger to his being tired after spending the morning trekking the serpentine trails.

The truth was, however, it was not fatigue that had brought him to his room, but disquietude. The confessions of LeMans and Harbley, far from giving him the feeling of relief expressed by the other guests, had tripped in his mind an even greater uneasiness than existed before. For some reason the events which had been described to him seemed inconsistent with the theories by which he judged human behavior. Perhaps he was being foolish to push his principles of economics into areas that were not traditional to the subject. Franklin Vincent certainly seemed to think so; Spearman remembered his painful meeting with the Cruz Bay detective. No doubt his colleagues in the economics department at Harvard would think he had gone overboard, as well. But the conversation Spearman had that morning with Matthew Dyke and Laura Burk prior to the nature walk suggested events that were at odds with his mode of analysis. Whenever anything of that nature occurred, his mind was focused on the problem until it was resolved.

Spearman opened the top drawer of the desk and retrieved a piece of paper from an envelope and spread it flat
before him. He knit his brows together as he pondered the
piece of stationery he had just unfolded. The professor
remained in this position for a long time. His only movement was a slow stroking of the chin. Spearman had committed the list of names on the paper to memory, but even
so he stared intently at each name on the roster as he
worked his way down the sheet. Then he pursed his lips
and, taking a pencil, carefully crossed through the names
of Ricky LeMans and Vernon Harbley. He put the pencil
down and resumed his concentration. So engrossed was
he in his thoughts that at first he did not hear his spouse
enter the room.

"I thought you'd be napping, darling."

To her surprise her husband did something uncharac-
teristic. He turned to her, got out of the chair, and began
to pace the room. "Pidge, I need your help. I want you to
go to the hotel's gift shop and get a cardboard box of these
approximate dimensions." He handed her a slip of paper
with the figures 4″ × 4″ × 6″ on it. "Also, I will need
enough brown wrapping paper and twine to wrap the box
and a shipping label to go on it. While you are doing that,
I am going to take a taxi into Cruz Bay, and I will meet
you here when I return."

In spite of her astonishment, Pidge was unable to
question her husband. She could see by his manner that
this strange request was of great importance to him. He
was out the door before she could even respond.

After returning from Cruz Bay and completing the
project in which he had enlisted his wife, Henry Spearman walked along the beach, a small brown package in
tow. He knew that the two people he wanted to find

would most likely be near the water on such a beautiful afternoon. And indeed they greeted him before he perceived their whereabouts.

"Professor Spearman, you ought to be in your bathing suit on such a nice afternoon!" Judy Clark called out from waist-deep water. Spearman waved a greeting to Mrs. Clark and her husband as he escalated his pace in their direction. "I have something for you!" he sang out.

"Just the people I've been looking for," he said as they emerged from the water. "I told the delivery man I would bring you this package personally since I figured you would be here on the beach."

"A package for us?" Mrs. Clark said quizzically.

"It's actually for you, according to the label," Spearman said, turning to Dr. Clark. "Here, I can see your hands are still wet; let me go ahead and open it for you." The professor had already begun undoing the twine as he said this.

"No, don't trouble yourself, Professor Spearman. We'll open it later," Dr. Clark protested.

"Oh, it's no trouble," he said, his hands busily unraveling the package.

"I said I'd do it," Douglas Clark replied in an imperious tone.

Spearman smiled back at him graciously, "But it's already done." The wrapping paper and box lay at his feet on the sand as he held up the package's contents. "It looks like somebody sent you a bottle."

Dr. Clark's eyes widened incredulously for a moment. He exchanged a darting glance with his wife who looked as amazed as her husband. Then he swung his hand out to take the object from Spearman's grasp.

Henry Spearman pulled the bottle away from the

doctor's reach. "Your hands are probably still wet; I'll read the label for you." Spearman held in his hand a small brown medicinal bottle with a white cap. He first appeared to read the inscription to himself and then announced to the Clarks: "According to the label, it's a poison—something called mephobarbital. I didn't see a return address on the package and there's nothing enclosed. Who do you think sent it to you?"

"How should I know?" Dr. Clark replied.

"Are you sure our name was on the package?" Judy Clark interjected as she bent over to pick up the wrapping. She stared at it for a moment and then showed it to her husband.

"It's addressed to me all right. But there must be some mistake. I never ordered any mephobarbital," Douglas Clark said cooly. By this time he had come in possession of the bottle, which he was inspecting with care.

"Well if you don't know who sent it to you, it may be some kind of prank. But if so, someone has a bizarre sense of humor. Mephobarbital, if my recollection is correct, is the poison that killed General Decker. I think we should call the police about this." Henry Spearman turned as if to lead the three of them towards the hotel.

Douglas Clark caught hold of his arm and restrained him. "I don't see why we should get the police involved in this. You're no doubt right, it's only a prank."

Spearman turned back to the Clarks. "Well, let's think about it for a moment." He paused as if to deliberate. "I guess maybe I am being rash. The police probably wouldn't be interested since they've caught Decker's murderers. For that matter the police might be a bit touchy toward anyone possessing mephobarbital after what happened here."

"That's right, Professor Spearman, there would just be a lot of questions about this silly prank," Judy Clark laughed nervously.

"But who would play such a crude joke on you? If you ever find out, you should certainly chastise them."

"I have some idea who did it, and if I find out I'm right, I will give them a piece of my mind."

Judy held the discarded wrapper against her bodice, and Doug, clutching the brown vial in his fist, motioned his wife in the direction of their cottage.

They had gone about six paces when Henry Spearman called back to them: "You know, perhaps I can help you out. The thought just occurred to me—it might be the same person who sent you the first package."

The Clarks stopped in their tracks. There was a moment's hesitation before the young physician spoke up. "What other package?" They were both still facing in the direction of their cottage and did not see the expression of mischief on Spearman's face.

"You know, the one you received about ten days ago."

The Clarks turned to face their agitator, and Dr. Clark sighed audibly. "I don't know anything about a first package."

"That's strange. The captain of the *Caribe Sun Rise* told me that you received just such a parcel on the sixth."

"We've never received any package off that boat. Captain Albin must be mistaken."

"Albin? It's curious that you know the captain's name."

"What are you getting at?" Judy Clark demanded. Her husband motioned her to keep still.

"I'm also curious," Spearman continued, "why you pretended to nightclub in Cruz Bay when all the while you were meeting the boat from Charlotte Amalie in expectation of a package. A package whose contents I am convinced ultimately led to General Decker's death."

"That's absurd. The murderers of General Decker have confessed and are behind bars. You know that yourself."

"Ah yes, the confessions. You must have been delighted with those. And since you probably aren't versed in game theory, you were doubtless surprised as well."

"Game theory? What on earth are you talking about?"

"Simple game theory—an ingenious device in the economist's toolkit. After I heard about the circumstances surrounding the confession of LeMans and Harbley, I realized that they were in a 'prisoner's dilemma,' one of the most basic stratagems in the theory of games. As Tucker showed, if two people are charged with a crime, and are separated by the police with no chance of their communicating, there are certain circumstances in which it would be rational for them to confess—even if they did not commit the crime. In economics this is called a dominant solution. I think LeMans and Harbley were in precisely that situation." Spearman went on to explain the conditions that would lead to a confession.

Under a prisoner's dilemma, if one prisoner confesses and implicates the other, while his partner remains silent, the confessor will receive a substantially lighter sentence than the one who denied the charge. The police in effect tell each prisoner separately that if he cooperates and confesses, his penalty will be reduced. If he doesn't confess, and his partner connects him with the crime, the book will be thrown at him. A second alternative is when neither confesses. Here there is a chance that both will be found guilty and receive heavy sentences, but this prospect has to be discounted by the possibility that each will be found innocent in the absence of implicating testimony. The final alternative is where both confess. In such a case, they will receive significant penalties, but not as severe as either would get for not confessing while the other did.

"So you see the dilemma, don't you? Even an innocent man, who feels the cards of circumstantial evidence or prejudice are stacked against him, has a great incentive to confess under these circumstances. For although he knows that they will both be better off if neither confesses than if both confess, he can't be certain that his cohort will plead innocent. So the safest strategy is for him to plead guilty, figuring his partner will do the same and against the chance that his partner might even plead innocent.

"And you think LeMans and Harbley are innocent because of an economic theory?" Dr. Clark ridiculed.

"The game matrix simply tells me that, guilty or innocent, they still would plead the way they did. But another tool in the economic theory kit tells me that you are guilty in the death of General Decker and that therefore LeMans and Harbley are innocent of this crime."

"Well if that theory is as complicated as your prisoner game, I don't think we care to hear it. Egghead theories don't carry much weight with me—or with anyone else outside of your ivory tower. And let me tell you another thing, Professor Spearman. I see now that your box incident was contrived. If you ever try something like that on me again, I'll push your face in. We're leaving in the morning, and I don't want to see you around before that time." Dr. Clark shook with anger.

"You're right about one thing," Spearman said in an

affable tone. "My theory about you does not seem to carry much weight with others. I began to explain it to Inspector Vincent sometime ago but fortunately, for your sake, he would not hear me out." Dejectedly Spearman left the beach. "Perhaps," he thought to himself, "if the police had seen Clark's reaction to an unexpected package, they would begin to place more faith in economic reasoning."

15

HENRY SPEARMAN had returned to his room following the confrontation with the Clarks. He relaxed somewhat, since an intellectual puzzle had fallen into place. The actions of the Clarks when confronted with the package were consistent with an earlier hypothesis he had formulated about them, and that fact cheered him considerably. He decided that he wanted to enjoy the afternoon air after experiencing what he considered to be a minor triumph. But there were still matters that weighed on his mind, and he was now encouraged to go on pushing his economics into criminology. Spearman took his folded list from the desk drawer and, putting a pencil in his pocket, exited the room. He began to stroll on the hotel grounds away from the beach. At first his wandering showed no particular intent. The professor was more concerned with turning certain facts over and over in his mind. He was persuaded, of course, that he had discovered the killers of General Decker and was now emboldened to think that by a similar process he might determine the killer of Justice Foote.

What did he know about the case? At first he had thought there must be a link between the two killings. Simple probability had made that seem likely. Now he wondered whether the improbable had not occurred. He could see no reason for believing that the Clarks were responsible for Foote's death. But if that were the case, who was? Perhaps it was a result of his reflecting on the death of the Justice, he was not sure, but eventually he found himself at the entrance to the Hawksnest trail. It was still not dusk, he thought to himself, so he decided to retrace the steps that the former justice had taken on that tragic afternoon.

As he proceeded up the path, he was glad that he had chosen to stroll here, since the proximity to the scene of the crime seemed to clarify his thought processes. Both the police and everyone he knew at the hotel seemed agreed that LeMans had a motive for killing the Supreme Court Justice. But did economic theory support their contentions?

The balding professor paused and stared at the list in his hand. Deliberately he drew the pencil from his pocket and placed the point next to the name of Ricky LeMans. His mind wrestled with a faint memory which was trying to surface. What was it that he had learned about LeMans which seemed pertinent here? Then it came to him, and he whispered to himself, "Of course, why didn't I think of that before." He wrote some numbers on the paper adjacent to LeMans's name: "150 = 1/2 × 300."

The principle is always the same, he thought. A rational person tries to achieve a given objective at the lowest cost or, what comes to the same thing, the greatest outcome at a given cost. In other words, it implies that people take account of their alternative opportunities. Once Spearman remembered that LeMans's musical services were more valuable on Saturday, he knew that

LeMans's guilt would be inconsistent with the theory of opportunity costs. For the Saturday afternoon concert LeMans received one hundred fifty dollars, which was pure gravy since bands did not ordinarily have afternoon engagements. When this was added to his income from the evening performances, the Saturday take at Cinnamon was two times what he could receive on any other day: three hundred versus one hundred fifty dollars. Consequently, for him to kill Foote it would have to be imagined that he had willingly foregone twice as much income as he would on any other day of the week. Since Foote was known to jog daily, it would be irrational for LeMans to choose to kill him at the very time he would lose the most income from missing a performance. If LeMans was the murderer, he could have committed the same crime at less cost to himself on any other day. That was enough to eliminate LeMans as a suspect in Spearman's mind. The bandleader's absence from the hotel that day, the economist predicted, would eventually be explained by some opportunity that LeMans valued even more than three hundred dollars.

Returning the pencil to his pocket, Spearman resumed his walk. He was now persuaded that LeMans had not killed Foote. And if LeMans was innocent of that crime, he reasoned, so was his subordinate Harbley, who took his orders from the bandleader. As he meandered along the trail, he reconstructed what he knew about each of the persons at the hotel who had some relationship with Curtis Foote.

Spearman stopped again when he realized that he was at the precise point where Foote had passed him the last time he saw the Justice alive. His breath stopped for a moment. Perhaps it was just his imagination, but for an instant he thought he heard those same footsteps in the distance.

Now it was unmistakable; they became louder. He braced himself against the kapok tree as if a Juggernaut were approaching. To Spearman's astonishment, the relentless figure coming upon him looked like Justice Foote. His heart pounded hard until he realized that his eyes were deceiving him. As the jogger came into view, Spearman was relieved to see that the person was not a ghost but only a guest whose stature resembled that of the late jurist.

When the jogger noticed Spearman, he slowed his pace and joked: "If you find me in the blowpipe, Doctor, please report it right away. At these rates I wouldn't want to pay for the extra night." He was obviously pleased with his quip and beamed as he swept by.

But if the jogger was hoping for a laugh from his audience, he was disappointed. Spearman had given him a disapproving look and said nothing. The young man taking his exercise thought that Spearman must be highly sensitive about the prominence he had attained at the hotel for having discovered the body of Justice Foote. Or perhaps he was still shook up by the event.

Getting his emotions under control, Spearman was a bit sorry he didn't respond more congenially to the first attempt at humor he had heard at the hotel in days. He could understand why the belief that the murderers had been caught could result in jesting. As a boy Spearman had observed the propensity of his relatives to quickly joke about and make light of dire circumstances from which they had just been delivered. But if the jogger had

known what Spearman had concluded about the innocence of LeMans and Harbley, he might not have found
things so funny. Indeed he probably would not have ven-
tured onto the Hawksnest trail.

The entrance to the dining hall was filling rapidly. On
Monday the dinner at Cinnamon was always a buffet.
And as usual the hotel guests arrived early. Not that any
shortage of food was envisioned. Quite the contrary; the
tables had to strain to support the bounty. What
prompted the early arrivals was the spectacle of it all. Platters of fresh fish and fowl were interspersed with giant
crystal bowls of fruits and vegetables. Each tray was garnished and arranged so that its contents blended with the
ice carvings and flowers which framed the buffet. At the
end of the table stood the chef himself. With knife in
hand, he presided over an enormous steamship round.
The appeal was as much to the eye as to the palate. Some
guests snapped pictures of the display, even though this
was known to be a *faux pas* at a hotel of Cinnamon's
caliber.

On this special night Henry Spearman and Pidge
donned the outfits that flattered them most. Mrs. Spearman wore a beige linen dress, and her husband had on a
powder-blue sport jacket and yellow slacks. They were
waiting in the queue among some younger guests whom
the Spearmans had overheard to be a group of nephews
and nieces vacationing at Cinnamon with their spouses at
the largesse of a wealthy aunt. The Spearmans had not yet
met anyone in this group, nor did the latter seem interested in making conversation with the professor and his

wife. The cousins were engaged in conversation among themselves about themselves.

Pidge Spearman stuck close to her husband's side. She was delighted that he had dressed for dinner and had even admitted to having an appetite. It had been her hope that Henry would begin to enjoy his vacation again after the confessions of LeMans and Harbley. But her husband not only failed to relax after this disclosure but actually seemed more preoccupied than ever with the events of the last few days. The wrapping of the box, she knew, was in some way connected with the homicides, although he had never explained to her precisely what it was he was about.

"If I didn't know better, I would think from watching you that the killers were still at large," Pidge Spearman stated to her husband.

"I don't know why you say that, dear. There were confessions."

"Henry, you're hiding something from me." She had been married to him long enough to know when something was on his mind.

Professor Spearman chuckled and then came clean. "I guess I have been elusive. But I didn't want to spoil your vacation. Everyone at the hotel seems so relaxed now, and I wanted you to enjoy yourself too."

"You know I can't enjoy myself when I know you're troubled. How do you always put it—our 'utility functions are interdependent'?"

Spearman put his arm around his wife's shoulder and gave her an affectionate hug. "If you talk like that, Harvard will have to give you a degree in economics—if not in economics, then in telepathy." He looked down at the floor for a moment and then admitted: "Actually I have been disconcerted over the confessions. The reason, I suppose, is fairly simple: I don't think LeMans and Harbley killed anyone."

"But they confessed and are in jail."

"That doesn't mean they are guilty."

"What more could you want?" Pidge Spearman objected. "That waiter could easily have poisoned General Decker. And remember, LeMans missed his performance at the hotel when Justice Foote was murdered and couldn't explain his absence."

"I can assure you that Harbley did not poison General Decker. What's more, I believe I know the likeliest person to have murdered Justice Foote."

"Who?"

"I would have to put my chips on Matthew Dyke."

Mrs. Spearman gasped. "You must be joking, Henry. He's a professor at Harvard."

"I believe there is a precedent for that," he said, reminding his wife of the case of Dr. John White Webster, the medical school professor who killed and dismembered one of Boston's most eminent citizens.

"But that was in the Medical School. Think of the scandal such a thing would cause in the Divinity School," she said.

"Then they may have to get set for a scandal," her husband warned.

"Why do you think Professor Dyke would do such a thing?" she asked, the look of incredulity still on her face.

Spearman mused about her question. He did not like to entertain queries which began with 'Why.' To him the interesting questions began with 'What.' An economist did not ask why a man prefers strawberry over vanilla but rather what his choice happens to be. It was for this reason that he considered his wife's question about Dyke's motives not nearly so pertinent as she might have imagined. Criminology, he had decided, concentrated too much on questions of motive. His training in economics had led him to believe that if he had to choose between two pieces of information in order to predict whether an individual was guilty or innocent, the person's motives or the person's choices before and after the crime, Spearman would always select the latter.

Mrs. Spearman interrupted her husband's reflecting. "Well, if you're right, that certainly eliminates the idea of Cynthia and Harold that that fellow Fitzhugh's drowning is related to the murder of Justice Foote."

"Yes, it does at that, doesn't it?" he mumbled, half to himself.

His wife, not hearing this, began again: "Now that you mention it, I believe I see why you think so. It's all that new morality business, isn't it? And, of course, those people he is always seen with. They've done terrible things, and he's always defending them, justifying with his philosophy their breaking the law. Even before Foote arrived, Professor Dyke had said what an evil man he was and how we would be better off if he were dead." Mrs. Spearman spoke emphatically, obviously pleased with herself for she thought she had been reasoning on her husband's wavelength. She was soon dissuaded of this.

"All of those things you say are true but irrelevant as they bear on my theory of his guilt."

Pidge looked disappointed. "What is *your* theory, Henry?"

"That people always buy more at lower prices," he replied.

"I know they do, but what does that have to do with Professor Dyke?"

He looked seriously into his wife's eyes. "What that has to do with Professor Dyke," he said slowly, "is simply this: Professor Dyke does not!"

At that point Mrs. Spearman again gasped. But not because of what her husband had just said. She had suddenly noticed that Professor Dyke, waiting only a few feet away, had been within earshot of their entire conversation.

16

"Now you see, Pidge, seventy cents for a fifteen-cent item is a perfect example of monopolistic pricing. The hotel is the only place on the island where out-of-town newspapers are available. The management is aware of this and, in maximizing profits, prices its merchandise accordingly."

The Spearmans were about to purchase their copy of the *New York Times* at the hotel's gift shop prior to having their breakfast. Ahead of them in line were two women wearing bathing shifts. One of them, a plump, middle-aged woman, was exclaiming in a loud voice: "I know it's time to go to breakfast, but I hardly enjoy eating anymore! It seems they are finding that everything that tastes good is bad for you. First it was milk and eggs, then it was cranberries, then coffee, and now they say nutmeg can be poisonous."

"Nutmeg?" her companion asked. "Don't tell me that. What will we sprinkle on our eggnog at Christmas?"

"I don't know, but there was an article in Saturday's *Times* which said doctors had found too much nutmeg was bad for you."

At breakfast that morning, Professor Spearman was even more preoccupied than usual. His wife noticed that he did not even order the fish of the day and that he was not reading his newspaper. Thus it was a surprise to her when he said, "How would you like to go away with me to our own little island—just the two of us?"

"Where?"

"Do you remember the small island we can see from our beach?"

"The one with all the gulls and pelicans flying around it?"

"Yes, he replied. "That island is called Henley Cay and I thought we could have the hotel pack us a box lunch and rent a boat to take us there this morning and pick us up later in the afternoon. We could spend the day beachcombing and exploring."

"Why, Henry, what a romantic idea!" Mrs. Spearman explained.

The waiter arrived with the rest of their order. When at home, Pidge Spearman did not eat a large breakfast, but she could not resist the fish of the day. Today's selection was yellow-tailed snapper. Mrs. Spearman particularly appreciated the fish with a side order of french toast, a dish which back home would seem too heavy for the morning meal. But she found the salt air made her appetite unusually keen.

Although Professor Spearman ordinarily preferred to have his seafood in the form of a shrimp omelette, which he consumed along with fried potatoes and coffee, today he was abstemious, ordering only juice and toast.

"There's your friend again, Henry!" Mrs Spearman remarked, delighted that her husband seemed to be in a holiday mood.

Henry Spearman looked up and watched the antics of

a pearly eyed thrasher which had alighted on the next table. Unlike the more cautious birds on the island, the mischievous thrashers took advantage of the open-air dining room and each morning pilfered scraps from vacated tables that had not yet been cleared.

"Look at how close he is to us," Mrs. Spearman said as the bird pecked at an English muffin. "I wonder why other kinds of birds don't fly in. There are so many tablescraps available it seems unfair that the thrashers get them all."

"Nothing unfair about it at all, Pidge. It is simply a matter of choice. The thrasher appears to have a preference for taking risks which other birds do not share." Spearman had once written an article delineating the importance of risk taking in a free-enterprise system and decrying the absence of this entrepreneurial spirit among contemporary businessmen. "Just like people, some birds are no doubt risk lovers, and others are risk averse. At any rate, we'd better not tarry over our breakfast or we'll run the risk of having our boat rented out from under us. I'd better hurry up and make the arrangements with the hotel for that and our lunch. Why don't you go back to the room and change into some hiking clothes, and I will meet you there shortly."

Professor Spearman walked from the dining area to the lobby and informed the hotel of his plans. The desk clerk looked disapprovingly at him when he heard of Spearman's proposed excursion.

"There's no problem renting a boat for the trip, Professor. Captain Blaylock can take you out there at ten this morning. But I can't guarantee a pleasant time for you on Henley. In the past that particular trip was planned as a regular excursion for our guests, especially the honeymooners who wanted to have an island all to themselves. But most people found the place rather unpleasant and desolate. And it turns out the island is a haven for scorpions and red ants. I wouldn't advise you to go, but if you really want to, I'll tell the captain and arrange for the kitchen to provide you and your wife with a box lunch."

"I appreciate the warning, but I think we'll go anyway. Please tell Captain Blaylock that he has two customers for a trip to Henley Cay." With that Spearman turned and hurried away.

The desk clerk stared at the departing figure in wonderment. It was the first time in his memory that the short professor had not bothered to make a searching inquiry into the price of a purchase.

But the desk clerk, had he been privileged to hear the professor's conversation with his wife the previous evening, would have been even more surprised at what happened next. For upon leaving the lobby, when Spearman happened to encounter the towering Matthew Dyke, he asked a favor of him.

"Professor Dyke, my wife and I want to spend a day by ourselves, so we have chartered a boat to take us to Henley Cay. It leaves in an hour. Would you be so kind as to remind the concierge to tell Captain Blaylock to pick us up at four this afternoon? I understand the island is quite desolate, and we don't want to be stranded there. Incidentally, since theologians enjoy solitude, the island might be just the place for you to visit sometime. Perhaps you ought to look into it."

"The contemplative life is not for me, Henry, but I will see to it that you're met there."

As it turned out, the Spearmans had not tarried too

long at breakfast. The boat they had secured through the hotel's concierge was ready promptly at ten o'clock, and soon after they were ensconced in the rear cushions of the launch as it made its way to the small, rocky island which sat about five hundred yards off Turtle Bay.

"I know I'm going to have a delightful time, Henry. I'm so glad you suggested this trip. But I must say I'm surprised you did so because recently you've seemed so preoccupied either with those murders or your economics."

"The two are not necessarily mutually exclusive," he said.

"Anyway, I'm relieved to be going some place where Professor Dyke isn't. Ever since he overheard us discuss our suspicions, I have been frightened that he might do something to us. Thank goodness he doesn't know where we are going."

"But he *does* know," Henry Spearman said. "I happened to mention our trip to him when I saw him after breakfast."

Pidge was momentarily astonished, for she thought her husband incapable of making such an obvious slip. "How could you tell him such a thing? He could come out here and kill us like he killed Justice Foote!" she exclaimed.

"There is no need to worry about that," her husband replied.

"Why? Only last night you thought he was a murderer."

"But that was the day before. Since then I have received new information which causes me to doubt the hypothesis that Dyke is the murderer. I *had* believed that he was guilty. Economic analysis pointed that way."

"How on earth could economics . . . ?"

"Let me show you. Remember how I indicated that Professor Dyke had done something very odd the night of the murder? He had seemingly violated the most fundamental tenet of all of economic theory: the law of demand."

"The law of demand?"

"Yes. You even agreed with me that everybody buys more at lower than higher prices. And I told you at the time that Professor Dyke does not. I had noticed that on every occasion, except at the manager's cocktail party on the day of the murder, Dyke obeyed the law of demand with textbook precision. On weekdays from five to six, when cocktails are at their lowest price, he drinks avidly and even purchases drinks for others. As the evening wears on and prices rise, his generosity decreases. He buys fewer drinks for others and for himself. The curious phenomenon that I observed at the manager's cocktail party was this: although Dyke's favorite beverage, planter's punch, was available at zero price, he drank far less of it than at any other time. In short, at a lower price he drank less than at a higher price. To me, that behavior required an explanation. I had decided that something had disrupted his normal pattern of life. The only apparent change in his environment was the murder of Curtis Foote. Therefore I concluded he was the most likely candidate to select as the murderer."

"Why have you changed your mind? What is different since that night?" his wife asked.

"Nutmeg."

Mrs. Spearman did not believe she had heard her husband correctly and inquired in disbelief. "'Nutmeg,' did you say?"

"Yes, nutmeg. On the day of the murder the *Times* carried an article explaining that the consumption of nutmeg could be poisonous. Now we know that Dyke reads the *Times* religiously. And we know that nutmeg is a prime ingredient in his favorite drink. A new hypothesis, therefore, presented itself. Professor Dyke's taste for planter's punch could have changed because of the nutmeg scare. That left me with two different hypotheses: Dyke radically altered his drinking behavior because of either murder or nutmeg. When an economist has two hypotheses which can explain the same thing, he is taught to choose the simpler explanation. In this case it is certainly the nutmeg."

As the boat approached the small dock on the east side of the island, Spearman stood up to watch the landing. His wife joined him at the starboard railing. "You know, Pidge, it's ironic, isn't it. Remember what I told you the other night about the murder at Harvard? In that case Professor Webster had deviated from his normal economic behavior by purchasing a huge turkey for the janitor of the building where he taught. He did this only a few days after the murder. This aberrant act of generosity on his part so set the janitor to wondering that he dug under Webster's lab and found parts of the body. The janitor was provoked by what I would call economic reasoning to solve a crime that had baffled the Boston police."

"But if economic reasoning tells you Dyke didn't kill Foote, does it tell you who did?" Mrs. Spearman asked.

Before he could reply, Captain Blaylock shouted back to them from the bridge: "We'll be docking now, and I'll leave you here for as long as you like. What time do you want me to return?"

"Promptly at four, please," Spearman answered. "We should be finished here by then."

Blaylock saluted in response and then piloted the launch alongside the wooden pilings of the dock. His mate helped the two passengers disembark from the craft while Blaylock kept the boat against the pier by deftly operating the engine and rudders. In this manner there was no need to tie the boat up during the brief stay. The mate handed the Spearmans their box lunch, and the two parties waved to one another as the vessel departed. Then the Spearmans turned to face the small island which was to be theirs for the day.

What they saw was not the prepossessing scene that travel agency brochures depict as a tropical island. Henley Cay consisted mainly of craggy rocks and boulders, scrub forest, and a plethora of native insects. The only distinguishing landmark of the island was a large tamarind tree on its eastern side.

Spearman turned to his wife and thought he could detect a slight look of disappointment on her face. "Not exactly my idea of where I would like to spend a second honeymoon, either," he said.

She looked back at him and smiled gamely. "I'm sure we will have fun together exploring. Besides, we haven't seen the whole island yet."

"Well, that won't be hard to do. It's only a half mile in diameter. Let's get started; perhaps we'll find a cool and scenic place by the time we're ready for lunch."

After about two hours of exploring, Spearman turned to his wife, "Let's sit down on this rock and rest a minute. A professor's life is too sedentary for sustained rock climbing in this temperature." Spearman took out a handker-

chief from his bermudas and mopped his brow. By mid-
morning the tropical sun was already intense, and they
both welcomed the pause in their explorations.

"Henry, you never did answer my question on the
boat."

"What question was that?"

"I asked you just before the boat landed if your economics tells you who killed Justice Foote. Do you know
who did it?"

"Pidge, you're always admonishing me about my
preoccupation with economics when I'm away from
Harvard," he ribbed her. "But since you brought it up, I
happen to have a hypothesis, and in fact I'm testing it
here."

His wife looked apprehensive as she asked, "What do
you mean, you're testing it here? If it's not Dyke or Le-
Mans, who else can you suspect?"

"Fitzhugh."

"But that's impossible. He's dead."

"That fact I have doubted for sometime. Do you remember when we first saw him? His behavior on the boat
at that time established not only his bigotry but also his
parsimony. I had further evidence of the latter that morning at the hotel when I got my fins. The hotel's rental
system should have appealed to a stingy man. For even
though the deposit on the fins is greater than their retail
price, the probability of losing the fins is so small that you
still are better off under their system than buying them."
Spearman paused. "Unless of course you are not expecting
to return the fins."

"But I still don't see how you knew . . ."

"With all the ruckus he made over having to put

down a deposit instead of being able to buy the fins outright, I decided Mr. Fitzhugh was not planning to return those fins. Later when I heard that he had drowned, I remembered the uncapped suntan lotion which he had left on the beach. Once again I thought it out of character for a stingy man to go in for a swim and be so careless with a bottle of lotion, leaving it where it could be easily spilled. Then I put together the two odd facts which puzzled me about him. Number one, he tried to buy his fins. Number two, the uncapped lotion. These two facts are consistent with his being stingy only under the hypothesis that he was not planning to return the fins or retrieve his lotion.

"But Harold and Cynthia thought he might have been forcibly drowned," Mrs. Spearman objected.

"But Pidge," he reminded, "you are forgetting the uncapped lotion. A man as stingy as Fitzhugh would be more cautious."

Mrs. Spearman thought for a moment. "Maybe he was dragged into the water before he could cap the lotion and then he was forcibly drowned."

"It would be foolish for a murderer to allow an intended drowning victim the advantage of putting on fins before forcing him into the water." Then Henry Spearman concluded: "So I began to think Fitzhugh was not dead but was only pretending to have drowned. When Curtis Foote was murdered, I suspected there might be a correlation between the drowning ruse and the death of the Justice."

"Well, then, I still don't understand why we are here."

"Because my hypothesis is that Fitzhugh swam here and used this island as a staging area for the murder. Any man who could swim to this island from our beach could easily reach the blowpipe, as well, and it is my hope today that we will find evidence that Fitzhugh was here."

"Not only *was*, but *is*," Bethuel Fitzhugh said as he emerged from behind a boulder brandishing a gun.

Mrs. Spearman gasped and grabbed her husband's arm. "Don't be so unhappy, Pidge," Spearman said to his wife. "After all, we've just seen my hypothesis confirmed. Albeit in a most unpleasant way."

17

STANDING BEFORE THEM, a grizzled beard all but hiding his surly features, was the person who had allegedly drowned. He looked different. He was no longer dressed in white, and his khaki clothes were tattered and soiled. His panama hat was gone and he had exchanged his white shoes for a pair of hiking boots. One might have mistaken him for an island beachcomber, but there was no mistaking the bulldog jaw.

"You know, you're a real piece of work," Fitzhugh said. "Since I seem to have stymied the police, I would have thought I could fool a Harvard professor. But you must not be the typical professor who is all wrapped up in theories."

"There is nothing wrong with theories, as long as they are sound," Spearman objected. He was more composed now and a bit riled at the ivory tower inference. "In fact it was economic theory that pointed to you as the murderer."

"I'm impressed, Professor. When I was in school, I thought economics was a bore. Maybe I should have studied it more carefully. But apparently the police are not taken with your theories. My friendly radio tells me that the police have fingered a couple of blacks as the perpetrators—as they say in the media."

Fitzhugh was beginning to warm up a bit. The Spearmans had startled him at first, but these gentle people could hardly be a real threat. He laughed, obviously beginning to enjoy the whole scene. "Tell me Professor, sir, what made you think I didn't drown? Everyone else seems to think I'm in some shark's belly by now."

Spearman must have realized how precarious his position was, but even so, he seemed almost happy to explain the rather involved rationale behind his deductions. Fitzhugh seemed fascinated as the professor demonstrated his powers of observation. Spearman told of the episodes on the boat with the tea, at the dock with the swim fins, and on the beach with the suntan lotion. Fitzhugh listened with amazement as he learned that his movements had been followed so closely. He could barely remember his one meeting with the professor on the beach just before the fake drowning. He was really astonished when the links between his actions and the murder of Justice Foote were pieced together by the articulate economist.

"That's really great. And it's true. But, how come you came here and not to the cops?"

"Well, it's like you said, the local police didn't buy my theories. I figured that I could substantiate my deductions if I could show that you were still alive. I fully expected to find evidence that you had been here on Henley Cay. I never imagined that you'd still be here."

"Well, you were a couple of hours away from being right on the nose with your deductions, since I'm leaving tonight. And I suppose you realize I can't afford to have your theories proved out."

Mrs. Spearman had recovered from the initial surprise, and as full understanding of their predicament dawned upon her, she felt faint. As she reached into her purse for her spirits of ammonia, Fitzhugh's arm shot out like a snake.

"Hold it, lady." He dumped the contents of the bag on the ground, and, seeing nothing menacing, he motioned for her to go about her business. Changing character abruptly, he turned his attention back to the professor, and almost pupil-like, he said, "I still don't see how you pegged me for knocking off Foote. The black guys confessed, and they're in jail. I don't get it."

Spearman was in his own element now. He was back in Cambridge addressing first-year graduate students. He skillfully led his student through the problems and the dilemma facing the unfortunate prisoners, concluding that the confessions are meaningless. Spearman explained the next part of the story almost as a classic case study, demonstrating that it was most unlikely that Le-Mans could have been the Saturday murderer. Any other day of the week would have offered the same opportunity without the economic loss.

Fitzhugh was captivated by the professor's logical deductions, but he had a question. "There was another murder before I got to the hotel. How come you couldn't figure that one out too?"

"But I did. And using simple economic theory once again."

"Well at least you can't pin that one on me."

You're right about that. It seems improbable but the two murders were committed by different murderers, and I can't find any connection. No, you didn't kill General Decker. The Clarks, Douglas and Judy, did that one."

Spearman had expected the exclamation of surprise

that emitted but he was not prepared for the look of amazed exasperation on the face of his captor. "Why do you find it so surprising that economic theory could solve that one too?"

Now it was Fitzhugh's turn to drop a bomb. "Yeah, I'm surprised all right. You see, Doug Clark is my brother. I'm Daryl Clark. Obviously I needed another name for the drowning scenario."

"I'm not really surprised. I figured all along that the two murders almost had to be related. The laws of probability and all that. I just hadn't noticed anything that tied the two together. You've done that, but I still don't see . . ."

"OK, Prof, we'll exchange hats and I'll tell the stories, since you seem so interested. The whole thing was a spur-of-the-moment deal. Doug and Judy had planned their vacation at Cinnamon for months. Finding Decker at the same hotel was a coincidence." Daryl Clark became menacing again as he told a story that had obviously been festering in his mind for some time.

"Doug and I had another brother. Much younger. Just a kid, really. He was killed in Vietnam in '72, and that bastard Decker was the commanding general over there at the time." Spearman interrupted:

"But certainly you can't blame the . . . "

"I'm the professor now, buster, and I know what you're thinking. The commanding general can't really be blamed for a second lieutenant getting killed, but this Decker wasn't your usual general. He took this war personally and often made decisions down at the company and sometimes even at the platoon level."

"Long after Doug and I buried what was left of our kid

brother, we learned from one of his buddies that that last search and destroy mission was strictly suicide. Decker was irritated because a particularly damaging enemy artillery position hadn't been destroyed. He left his sumptuous quarters in Saigon and went to the front. He ordered the first platoon he came upon to attack the position. It finally took ten platoons along with air support to wipe out that position. Doug and I checked out the story with other sources. It was true, and right then we vowed to get Decker if we ever had the chance. Well now, here he was, handed to us on a silver platter.

"Doug had me send down some poison, which did the job just fine, as you know. Trouble was, Doug overheard a conversation indicating that this Foote person may have seen him do it. That's when I came down to help Doug with the plan he worked out. It was easy. I'm a strong swimmer, and Doug learned the judge's jogging routine. Doug and Judy will pick me up tonight, and tomorrow Daryl Clark will be back in the States and the lightly lamented Fitzhugh gone to his reward. I think it's just great that the police have solved these terrible crimes. We wouldn't want to spoil things, would we now?"

With Clark bringing up the rear, this unlikely trio made their way along a stoney, root-studded path to the north side of the island. The narrow trail circled below the island's large tamarind tree and was overgrown with scrub brush which made the traversing of it arduous. Because it was midday, the tropical sun's rays were so intense that Mrs. Spearman felt faint again, though she was not certain whether it was from heat or from fear.

The trail led to a promontory overlooking the channel. There the trio stopped. It was an unlikely sight in which to feel the grip of terror. In the distance pleasure craft split the azure Caribbean waters, and seagulls skimmed the whitecaps. But the Spearmans were oblivious to the incongruity of the scene; their attention was occupied by the lethal weapon which Clark had trained upon them.

Clark intended no further conversation. He saw no problems. No one would hear the shots, and the bodies would fall into the water below to find the same fate as the mythical Fitzhugh. Henry Spearman could read the confidence in Clark's eyes.

"It won't be that easy for you."

"You're dreaming, Professor. I've been swimming down below. Those currents are murder—you should excuse the expression." Spearman was desperate now—knowing that he and his wife were probably doomed, but knowing also that as long as he could keep the conversation going, then at least they would be alive. Something might happen.

"You've forgotten the man who brought us out here. He'll come to pick us up soon, and when we're not waiting on the dock, he'll look all over this island. He'll probably find you, or at least some indications that you were here. You can't keep killing everyone who gets in your way. You're bound to stumble. Why don't you . . ."

Henry Spearman never had a chance to suggest an alternate plan. Clark had lost his awe for Spearman's deductive reasoning, and he was concentrating on covering his departure for the States that evening. As he spoke, it was more thinking out loud than in answer to Spearman.

"Forget it, Professor. Let's see now, I'll simply leave a note for the boat captain. You've changed your plans and begged a ride with some folks in a passing sailboat. You'll pay the captain for his troubles either this evening or to-morrow morning. Your being among the missing probably won't be discovered until tomorrow and I'll be safely away. All wrapped up, pat and beautiful." Clark went on, almost musing to himself. His words were confident, but a tone of doubt began to creep into his voice.

"You know, it's almost funny, it's so perfect. I've never been here. The person I was is presumed dead. Perfect." The professor noticed the hesitation. Why didn't Clark use that gun? What was he waiting for? Could this man be squeamish about doing away with a man and his wife while looking at them face to face? After all, he had per-sonally murdered Justice Foote. Henry Spearman wasn't ready to give up, even though he probably could not stall Clark for the full hour before Captain Blaylock would return in the launch.

"Why . . . why do you use an automatic instead of a revolver?" Pidge Spearman hardly understood the inane question. She was almost in a state of shock. The fact that Clark answered the question showed that he too wel-comed a chance to collect his resolve to do what he must for his own survival.

"Revolver, automatic. I don't know. Why do some tennis players use metal rackets instead of wood? There's just something about a revolver that . . ."

He never finished the sentence. A second before he screamed, his face contorted in agony. He dropped the gun as he rolled to the ground, beating at his legs. Henry Spearman had no idea what was happening, but he went for Clark's gun immediately. Pidge watched in shock and then horror as Clark, still screaming, tore at his pants like a madman. Where he had torn them away, Pidge saw tiny red objects on his skin. Almost like a rash, but they were moving.

Clark had been standing on the nest of a colony of tropical army ants. These tiny but vicious creatures had crawled up his legs and then, as if on a signal, they attacked, their instinctive trait telling them that their forces were deployed and ready. Had Clark been tied down, or wounded, he might have lived no more than an hour. As it was, in a few minutes he made some progress in ridding himself of the tiny red monsters.

The pistol now felt comfortable in the professor's hand as he watched Clark's wild antics begin to become more systematic. In about ten minutes he had scraped off the last of the ants and turned his attention to the larger scene. He had so concentrated on the ants that he seemed almost surprised that the situation had turned completely around. Full realization came as he finally focused on the gun in Spearman's hand. It was pointed at his chest. Though the two men were a good ten feet apart, Clark made a move to close the gap.

"Hold it right there." The professor's voice had an astonishingly strong quality for all of his small physical stature. Clark stopped in his tracks. "And don't get any further ideas. While you were frolicking with those delightful red ants, I found the safety catch on this thing, and it's definitely off and ready to fire."

Spearman went on, the relief showing in his voice. "I have still another theory for you, Mr. Clark. At this range, I don't think I could miss your chest. And I probably could get off two or three shots before you reached me. The way to test this new theory of mine is for you to take a step in any direction."

It was over. Captain Blaylock arrived on time, and they headed for Cruz Bay instead of Cinnamon, where Spearman's prisoner was turned over to the police. Clark confessed immediately and Franklin Vincent called Aberfield to have him make arrangements to apprehend Judy and Doug Clark.

Vincent was full of apologies, which Henry Spearman shrugged off with obvious pleasure. Inspector Vincent's open-mouthed amazement at the professor's ability to solve the Cinnamon Bay murders amused the economist, and he couldn't resist saying, "Elementary, my dear Vincent. Elementary economics, that is." Pidge Spearman, having recovered most of her composure, was slightly embarrassed at her husband's remark.

Later, in Vincent's office, Henry Spearman looked and sounded more and more like an economics professor, even though his antics of that day might be more in keeping with a John Wayne portrayal. With his short legs dangling just above the floor as he sat and his cherubic face almost shining, he told Vincent the story of his deductions. He explained how he made use of economic concepts of opportunity costs, the prisoners' dilemma, the law of demand and capital and how all of these worked together to determine the inconsistencies in the actions of Daryl Clark alias Bethuel Fitzhugh and how these led him to Henley Cay. He described how close he and his wife had come to death.

It was too much for Inspector Franklin Vincent. "You lost me in your theories, Professor, but let's just say I followed you all the way. There's still something I'll never understand. How did you ever come to suspect the Clarks in the first place? I never saw a more typical, open, honest and attractive couple ever come to these islands."

The professor's pique surfaced as he explained. "I tried to tell you about that when I first came over here and you wouldn't listen. It was the law of demand at work. This is a law that will not be broken, and yet they broke it—the most firmly entrenched principle in the whole fabric of economics. I tried to tell you about the Clarks because I simply could not conceive of this law not working.

"Let me run through the story again quickly. Now that you know the end of the story, you might be ready to accept the truth of its beginning. When the Clarks first came to Cinnamon, they came over here to Cruz Bay for the nightclubs every evening, or so they said. Why did they come over here? Because it was cheaper than the evening entertainment at the hotel, even with cab fare. Once again, so they said." Henry Spearman was in his element. He was on his feet now and pacing back and forth in front of his audience. He was back in Cambridge again, but this time in the undergraduate school addressing freshmen.

"Now. When the Clarks' children were sent home to visit their grandparents, the pattern of their behavior changed abruptly. From that point on, they stayed at the hotel for the evening instead of coming over to Cruz Bay." Vincent had been following Spearman's narrative closely and nodded his head at each thought. But now, the blank look returned.

"Hold it a minute, Professor. You told me all this before and I still can't see why you became suspicious of the Clarks when the kids went home."

"Inspector Vincent, didn't I see a blackboard in your outer office? If that could be brought in, perhaps I could show you how some numbers would substantiate my deductions and confirm my suspicions." The blackboard was brought in and Spearman stood before it seeming even more in his own environment, if that were possible.

"All right, let's establish one truth. The Clarks spent their evenings in Cruz Bay to save money right? Right. Let's look at the cost." At this point Spearman began writing on the blackboard in that backhanded way teachers use so that they don't block out what they're writing.

	Cruz Bay
Nightclubbing plus cab fare	$14
Babysitter	4
Total	$18

After putting the figures on the board the professor smiled again and wrote.

	Cinnamon Bay
Entertainment cost at the hotel	$30
Baby sitter	4
Total	$34

89% higher than at Cruz Bay

"Now the Clark children are shipped home. This eliminates the babysitting expense. At this point Spearman crossed out the $4 for babysitting and entered a new total of $14 at Cruz Bay and $30 at Cinnamon. Now, we have a new cost differential." Whereupon the professor crossed out the 89% and wrote in 114%.

"Yet even with this relative increase in the price of the hotel—we're comparing a one hundred and fourteen percent difference to an eight-nine percent differential—the Clarks opted for the hotel. They should have done just the opposite. While both spots became cheaper in absolute terms, in relative terms Cruz Bay became even less expensive. So I knew something was wrong here. There had to be some explanation for this illogical and uneconomic behavior in which the Clarks demanded less of something after it became cheaper." Spearman had his audience in the palm of his hand now and he knew it. He moved the blackboard out of the path of his pacing route.

"And other happenings began to weave into this pattern of inconsistency. The Clarks switched their nightclubbing to Cinnamon on the very night that General Decker was killed. This was the night that Doug and Judy Clark should have been over here in Cruz Bay, according to the law of demand. That's why I came over to see you, Inspector, but you wouldn't listen." Inspector Vincent squirmed in his seat appearing precisely like a freshman who went to a beer party instead of doing his homework. Precisely, that is, if you overlooked the lines in his face and the thinning hair. The professor bore on, oblivious to Vincent's uneasiness.

"When I saw that you were not going to take any action, I decided to perform a test of my own to learn the true reason for the Clarks' excursions to Cruz Bay."

Spearman then told of his visit to the dock and the inquiries made there. He explained with a relish his charade with the package he had prepared to test the Clarks' reactions and how these had confirmed his suspicions.

"So. We learn from these exercises that every law officer should be trained in economic theory. Right, Inspector?" The professor didn't really expect an answer. Inspector Vincent was sitting there sort of slumped down and still shaking his head in disbelief. Even though the power of economics had been demonstrated beyond question, Spearman had the feeling that criminal investigation methods were not going to change—at least not in this part of the Caribbean.

The next morning as the Spearmans prepared to depart for St. Thomas and their flight home, they were moved by the presence of Vernon Harbley, Ricky LeMans, and his mother, who had come to the dock to thank Professor Spearman and wish them good-bye. Henry Spearman shyly received their appreciation and seemed particularly pleased to have an opportunity to see LeMans before he returned to Cambridge. In his mind there was still a part of the mystery which was as yet unresolved. LeMans was the only one who could satisfy his curiosity on this point. Taking hold of the bandleader's arm and walking away from within earshot of the others on the dock, Spearman said in a soft voice: "You can be assured of my complete discretion. I presume that your absence from the hotel when Justice Foote was killed must be explained by an opportunity of more value to you than the income you lost as a result of your missing your scheduled engagement here. Yet you did not explain your whereabouts to the police. My nature is such that I am troubled if a theory of mine lacks supportive evidence. You asked me a moment ago if there was any way you could reciprocate for what I've done. I would appreciate knowing what caused you to forego three hundred dollars on that particular Saturday when you were absent from the hotel."

"Four hundred dollars."

"But if you earned four hundred dollars elsewhere, why didn't you use that as an alibi?"

"I got four hundred dollars that day from a brother who's very important to our movement. I couldn't tell the police I'd been with him because they might have tracked him down."

"That completes the puzzle," Spearman said.

As the Spearmans settled onto the cushioned benches of the hotel's launch, Walter Wyatt, the manager of Cinnamon Bay, came aboard to express the hotel's appreciation. "Here's something you might enjoy reading on the trip back," he said, showing them the morning newspaper from Charlotte Amalie which had headlined the capture of the Clarks by the local police on St. Thomas. The front page of the paper prominently displayed a picture of the young couple handcuffed to a beaming police officer. The picture's caption read, "INSPECTOR ABERFIELD SOLVES CINNAMON BAY MURDERS." At about the same time in Cruz Bay, Inspector Franklin Vincent was reading the same story with remarkable lack of enthusiasm.

Captain Blaylock was at the helm as the hotel launch churned into Pillsbury Sound. Later, as the boat headed toward Red Hook landing at St. Thomas, Pidge Spearman broke the pleasant silence that had lasted the entire trip thus far.

"Well Henry, we'll soon be on the plane back to Boston."

"Yes, and then I can get back to thinking about economics." He sounded serious but his eyes were smiling.

WHY WOULD two mainstream economists experiment with the detective novel genre as a vehicle for presenting their ideas? This is a personal account of the history of *Murder at the Margin*: the genesis of our economist-sleuth, the writing of his first adventure, our search for a publisher, and some consequences of the book's appearance. For objectivity and convenience, the story is told in the third person.

To William Breit and Kenneth G. Elzinga, it seems only yesterday that they sat down to write the first Spearman adventure. They had been vacationing at a posh hotel (during off-season rates) on the island of St. John. Breit had carried along a stack of mysteries for summer reading and he was brazen enough to think that he might be able to write a book as good as some of those he had brought to the Caneel Bay Plantation hotel.

The seed for such an idea had in fact long been gestating in Breit's mind. He had been an admiring fan of Harry Kemelman's Rabbi Small series, which started with *Friday the Rabbi Slept Late* in 1964, in which murders are solved through the Rabbi's knowledge of the Talmud. It occurred to Breit, a voracious reader of mystery fiction, that "whodunits" had a wide variety of characters in the role of amateur detective: G. K. Chesterton had Father Brown, the Catholic priest; Agatha Christie had Miss Marple, the spinster of St. Mary Mead; Rex Stout had Nero Wolfe, the obese orchid grower who seldom left his Manhattan

brownstone. Why not, thought he, an economist as detective who uses economic theory to solve crimes? Since
the mastermind sleuth must be the most rational of all
creatures, one might surely be an economist. Economics,
after all, is the social science that has as its main actor a
rational calculating *homo economicus.*

One evening, while strolling back from the dining
room, Breit casually mentioned the thought to Elzinga,
his friend and fellow economist. Elzinga surprised him by
his enthusiasm for the idea. He challenged Breit to try his
own hand at writing such a novel. The latter demurred:
the opportunity costs would be large, requiring many
hours that could be spent on serious economics. Elzinga
countered: writing such a murder mystery would not be an
alternative to doing economics, but an alternative way of
dealing with the subject. Breit objected, admitting to a
character flaw: he could be dragged to the movies at almost any moment at anyone's urging. Elzinga offered an
inducement: they would attempt it together. The genes
inherited from his Dutch forebears had provided Elzinga
with the discipline Breit lacked. Persistence won: Breit
was persuaded. Together they would test his idea in the
crucible of collaboration.

Breit impressed upon Elzinga the importance of a distinctive protagonist. To be memorable, fictional sleuths
must be eccentric characters with unusual personalities.
Their foibles are remembered long after the plots of the
novels in which they appear are forgotten. Eventually the
pair chose as their prototype Milton Friedman, the economist's economist. Friedman thinks in economic terms
about almost everything and his short stature, bald head,
easy smile and brilliant mind seemed ideal traits for a fictional character. Moreover, by chance many of his char-

acteristics are the opposite of those of Sherlock Holmes, the most famous fictional sleuth. In physique, Milton Friedman is short, Sherlock Holmes is tall; in personality, Friedman is cheerful and smiling, Holmes is stern and gloomy; in lifestyle, Friedman is happily married, Holmes is a confirmed bachelor.

And so Henry Spearman was born. This name was chosen because it is similar in cadence and inflection to that of "Milton Friedman"; it has the ring of perceptiveness and finality to it—as does a spear piercing to the heart (of a problem); and its initials are the inverse of those of Arthur Conan Doyle's creation. Possibly the name of Nobel Prize winner Kenneth Arrow also had some influence on the selection. It was quickly decided that the book would be written in the tradition of the British cerebral mysteries, the so-called "cozies," rather than in the style of the hard-boiled detective fiction of Dashiell Hammett and Raymond Chandler. Nor would there would be graphic violence and fast-paced action á la Robert Ludlum. Rather it would be in the spirit of Agatha Christie, with Henry Spearman a kind of professorial Hercule Poirot.

In such literature an exotic or intriguing setting is obligatory, ideally one which is cut off from the outside world by storm, water, or jungle. Typically, the only inhabitants of this universe are the detective, victims, suspects, police, and murderer. Breit and Elzinga realized that their vacation hotel fit the bill perfectly. Caneel Bay Plantation, a resort on the smallest of the American Virgin Islands, was a little world all to itself. It boasted two open-air dining pavilions with excellent kitchens, comfortable cottages, and seven white sand beaches bordering blue water of transparent clarity. The grounds of well-tended lawns, coconut palms, and flowering gardens were surrounded by thick tropical foliage through which a few rock-strewn hiking paths had been hacked. At places these paths wound their way along steep cliffs that dropped precipitously into the roaring surf. There was an eeriness about these lonely paths that had not escaped Breit and Elzinga's notice. In addition, among the hotel's guests and employees were some colorful characters who could serve as prototypes for victims and suspects. It was agreed that Henry Spearman's adventure would be set at just such a place, renamed Cinnamon Bay Plantation.

The next order of business was the choice of a joint pseudonym. To use their own names had disadvantages: Breit and Elzinga had collaborated already on a few articles in the professional journals of economics and law. It seemed sensible to separate all previous and future nonfiction efforts from their foray into fiction. In addition, there was ample precedent for jointly authored mystery novels to appear under a single pseudonym. Ellery Queen was in actuality two cousins, Frederick Dannay and Manfred B. Lee. Emma Lathen was two Boston women, Martha Hennisart and Mary J. Latsis. The team of Adelaide Manning and Cyril Coles wrote under the name of Manning Coles. Francis Beeding was two Englishmen, John Leslie Palmer and Hilary Adrian St. George Saunders. Breit and Elzinga, after playing with some possible candidates, settled on "Marshall Jevons," the surnames of two nineteenth-century English economists (Alfred Marshall and William Stanley Jevons) who pioneered the use of marginal analysis.

Having determined the name and personality of their detective, the setting of their story and their joint pseudo-

nym, Breit and Elzinga turned their attention to the construction of their plot. They understood from the beginning that in order for Marshall Jevons to find a niche in
the field of detective fiction he would need an original
ploy upon which the unravelling of the mystery would
depend. Early on it was decided the solution would hang
on a well-established "law" of economics. But the principle would be explained unobtrusively early in the book,
only to reappear surreptitiously in a totally different con-
text later, where it would be the key to Henry Spearman's
solution of the murders. To be effective, the economic
principle would have to be one that sounded plausible
and simple upon first exposure to the reader, but one that
had a "hidden logic"—that is, far-reaching implications
that were not obvious on the surface. What could be more
plausible than the law of demand (at lower prices people
will buy more of a commodity than at higher prices)? Yet
the implications of the law of demand are subtle. Understanding them is what enables Spearman to unmask the
culprits at the end of the novel. Spearman's method of
deduction would be the most distinctive feature of the
book.

Once Breit and Elzinga found the appropriate economic gimmick, they could struggle with the develop-
ment of their plot. Understanding the importance of veri-
similitude in mystery fiction, they researched relevant as-
pects of the Virgin Islands: its geology; its flora; the exotic
fish in the Caribbean; the making of a steel drum for use
by a steel band; the kind of police cars used by the St.
John's police force; the police station in Cruz Bay; local
foods; and the kind of boats that run from St. Thomas to
St. John. Together they worked on almost every sentence,

trying out various possible phrasings on each other before adding the chosen words to the yellow pad. The novel took three years to complete, the time made long by the episodic attention they could give to the task. Breit and Elzinga had other commitments, and in the interim they wrote a book on antitrust penalties and contributed articles to professional journals.

Murder at the Margin was completed in settings far removed from the one in which it was begun: in Elzinga's study on his small farm near Keswick, Virginia, and in Breit's house near Charlottesville. It was in Breit's study by a window with a view of a lawn that sloped down to some elms lining the banks of a small stream where they agreed upon the final pages. It was an exhilarating moment.

Writing a book is one thing; getting it published is another. The first obstacle was not having a literary agent. Without a literary agent they could not get into a publishing house. That had never been a problem for them in the past. Publishing books on technical economics does not require an agent.

Breit and Elzinga sent the manuscript for *Murder at the Margin* to a number of publishers only to have it back by return mail unopened with an appended note about not receiving manuscripts "over the transom." They tried to hire a literary agent and found themselves in a classic Catch-22. A literary agent with clout enough to get into a publisher's office won't sign up an unpublished and unknown fiction writer.

Then one day Thomas Horton, owner of a small publishing house specializing in economics and business texts, walked into Breit's office at the University of Virginia. He asked about the possibility of Breit adopting one of his textbooks. His firm, Thomas Horton and Daughters, published Milton Friedman's *An Economist's Protest* and Paul Samuelson's *The Samuelson Sampler*, compilations of selected *Newsweek* columns that the two Nobel economists had written. When Breit inquired about how to get a publisher for *Murder at the Margin*, Horton replied he had always had an interest in publishing fiction, and that he had an appointment to see Samuelson at MIT the following week. "I trust his judgment," he said. "I'll ask him to read your manuscript. If he recommends that I publish it, I will." As it turned out, Samuelson liked the book and so did his mystery-buff secretary.

When the book appeared there was no indication on the dust jacket of the true identity of Marshall Jevons (although it would not have been hard to find out for anyone in circulation among academic economists). Instead, for the "About the Author" section on the cover's back flap, Elzinga concocted a biographical statement projecting a version of a life that fulfilled both authors' ultimate fantasies:

> Marshall Jevons is the President of UtilMax, Inc., an international consulting firm headquarted in New York City. A former Rhodes Scholar, he holds advanced degrees in economics, biochemistry, and oceanography. Mr. Jevons is an Olympic medal holder in kayaking whose hobbies now include rocketry and the futures market in cocoa beans. He is a native of Virginia but prefers to call 'home' the Queen Elizabeth 2. This is Marshall Jevons' first novel.

Almost simultaneously with the appearance in hardcover of *Murder at the Margin* in the late summer of 1978, an exceedingly kind review in the *Wall Street Journal* gave the book much favorable publicity. Fortuitously, the *New*

York Times was on strike, a fact that increased the circulation of the *Journal* considerably. Under the heading, "Henry Spearman, the Chicago School Sleuth," John R. Haring, Jr. hailed the work for its educational and entertainment value, saying, "if there is a more painless way to learn economic principles, scientists must have recently discovered how to implant them in ice cream." This review, which revealed the not-so-secret secret of Marshall Jevons's identity, got the book off to a good start. Orders from bookstores, especially in New York, poured into Thomas Horton and Daughters. Sales were brisk, and picked up more as the book began to find a niche as a supplement to textbooks in introductory economics courses. Other reviews, in the professional journals of economics, were mostly favorable, although there were detractors. One of them was David Friedman, the son of Milton Friedman, who wrote a criticism in a review article in *Public Choice*. Under their pseudonym, Breit and Elzinga contributed a reply. There was no rejoinder from Friedman.

To Breit and Elzinga, the most surprising and gratifying aspect of publishing their novel was the fan letters it generated: a few arguing about the solution to the puzzle, some discussing technical details, others merely wanting to express their compliments. This side benefit was not expected since fan mail, especially from noneconomists, had not been forthcoming after the publication of their nonfiction works. The mail gave reassuring evidence that people actually had read the book and enjoyed it, or at least took it seriously enough to take the trouble to write.

One of the first letters received was from Milton Friedman himself who saw through the roman á clef. "Delighted to have played a role unknowingly and indirectly in the book," he wrote. Another letter came from a reader in Yoakum, Texas, who gently but firmly informed the authors that automatics, not revolvers, have safety catches—one of the few corrections they took the liberty to make in the present edition. Especially agreeable was a letter from an economist in Pittsburgh who wanted to express her gratitude to Marshall Jevons. It seems her non-economist husband found it difficult to communicate with her because he was baffled by her way of thinking. She gave him a copy of *Murder at the Margin* and their marriage was saved. Possibly the most perceptive letter came from Kaye D. James, a graduate student at Vanderbilt University, who prior to reading the novel was acquainted with an article by Breit and Elzinga in the *Journal of Law and Economics*. While reading the murder mystery, the name Arvel Blaylock, the skipper of the Grand Banks trawler for the Cinnamon Bay Plantation, seemed familiar. The observant student was right. In the article, Arvel Blaylock is named as the owner of the Russellville Canning Company in Russellville, Arkansas, who sued the American Can Company in a precedent-setting antitrust case. Breit and Elzinga borrowed Blaylock's name and assigned it to their fictional sea captain, never dreaming their ruse would be discovered. The most controversial letter, charging Marshall Jevons with "sexism," came from an intermediate microeconomics class at a small college in Ohio. The professor and students were particularly upset by the character of Pidge Spearman, who in the novel is treated as being intellectually inferior to her husband. In reply, Marshall Jevons politely rejected the accusation, pointing out that Henry Spearman is depicted as being more intelligent than anyone else at Cinnamon Bay, male or female. Just as Sherlock Holmes needed Dr. Watson as a foil for his speculations and discoveries, Henry Spearman found his Watson in the person of his wife, Pidge. This literary device has the inevitable result of making the sleuth's companion, male or female, appear somewhat slow compared to the hero.

The success of *Murder at the Margin* led MIT Press to approach Breit and Elzinga about the possibility of writing a sequel. It would be the first work of mystery fiction to be published by a university press. The offer could not be resisted and so Henry Spearman returned in 1985 in *The Fatal Equilibrium*. One year later Ballantine issued it as a mass market paperback. Marshall Jevons was soon to discover that there are few pleasures more satisfying than seeing one's own paperback in a book rack at an airport newsstand. After translation, the book became a best seller in Japan where fifty thousand copies were sold within the first few months of its publication.

What next for Marshall Jevons? It is too early to announce his forthcoming *chef-d'oeuvre* in which Henry Spearman once again demonstrates the power of economic reasoning to foil a diabolical villain. Suffice it to say that, however many new experiences of the amateur sleuth Jevons chronicles, there will always be a special place in his heart for Henry Spearman's debut adventure, where the diminutive professor encounters and resolves the mysterious affair at Cinnamon Bay.

Marshall Jevons
April 1, 1993